Changes of Address

Changes of Address

A Novel by

LEE LANGLEY

COLLINS
8 Grafton Street, London W1
1987

William Collins Sons & Co. Ltd
London · Glasgow · Sydney · Auckland
Toronto · Johannesburg

BRITISH LIBRARY CATALOGUING IN PUBLICATION DATA

Langley, Lee
Changes of address.
I. Title
823'.914[F]   PR6062.A5335

ISBN 0-00-223234-0

First published 1987
Copyright © Lee Langley 1987

Photoset in Linotron Palatino by
Rowland Phototypesetting Ltd
Bury St Edmunds, Suffolk
Made and Printed in Great Britain by
Robert Hartnoll (1985) Ltd, Bodmin, Cornwall

For Fabio Mataloni

Part One

Often it begins with a telegram, this process of looking back. A telegram bringing news of a marriage, a birth, a death. And there *was* a telegram, but that was much later. So I will begin not with the telegram, nor with the jazz song that played its part, nor with a certain monsoon or the magic which I believed in, always. I should begin, perhaps, with the men.

My mother knew the man who wrote *The Green Hat*. She knew the Maharaja of Jaipur, a sculptor with Lalique connections, a *Luftwaffe* pilot with duelling scars, and the man who ran the Brighton Aquarium. These, and others like them, she knew socially, glancingly. She encountered them at cocktail parties and receptions; on ocean liners, at the opera, in hotel lounges, on the beach.

Others she knew on a more personal footing: a Scottish tea planter, a Norwegian sea-captain, several officers and NCOs in His Majesty's armed forces; a US Army colonel from Chicago. There was also an able-bodied seaman whose face I never saw but whose beard and pubic hair, glimpsed through an open bedroom door, glittered bright ginger. Him she knew for a day.

In various ways and in varying degrees of intimacy, my mother was acquainted with many men.

But the men, though they figured large, came later. At the beginning there was no one else, so I see that there is only one way to begin: with her.

*

She described her hair as tawny: it had strands of auburn intermingling with dark brown and mouse. Depending on the time of day and social requirements it could be a greasy tangle or a sleek, tigerish pelt.

She was tall, with prominent, equine features, a straight back, small breasts and high, rounded haunches. She had beautiful hands and feet. Proud of her arched instep she wore very high heels, and perhaps because these threw her pelvis into an unnatural position she had a stalking, loping stride which gave her the appearance of a huntress on the prowl. She had a certain Thirties look: large eyes, surprised eyebrows, fine-grained white skin. Her legs were good – photographers occasionally used her to model silk stockings or shoes.

I saw a picture in *Vogue* once, not in the high-fashion editorial pages but up front among the advertisements. It was a quarter-page shot of a woman descending a staircase, and all you could see were the legs and feet, foreground, to show off the stockings. That was my mother. Or so she said.

On good days the grey-green eyes were bright, the spine straight; the wide, thin-lipped mouth curved in a smile inviting misbehaviour and complicity. At other times she could be baleful. Ugly.

We travelled a lot, she and I. Whole days and nights on trains; weeks at sea. We had two big trunks and several suitcases of heavy leather. She had hat-boxes, at the start. Gradually, as things changed, so did the luggage. It dwindled.

I was old for my age. And for good reasons: she had decided that a nine-year-old child was acceptable – just – in her social scene. Anything more advanced in years would be an embarrassment: my growing older aged her.

'Of course, I had the Child when I was just twenty,'

she would say. But she refused to allow me to thrust her into her thirties. She remained credibly twenty-nine while I was nine. I was nine – 'just nine' – for quite some time.

'Such a great, strapping girl!' she would exclaim, amused, dismayed, shrugging slim shoulders. I had heavy shoulders, inherited from my father. A slouch. A chubby body. I was, in fact, small, for ten and a half.

It was depressing, being held at nine indefinitely; I felt imprisoned and would ask from time to time, 'Couldn't I have a birthday soon? Couldn't I be ten?' My mother was adamant. Just nine.

'Yes, a big girl, I'm afraid.'

My mother possessed two books – Boccaccio's *Decameron* and Fitzgerald's translation of *The Rubáiyát* of Omar Khayyám – and one record: Billie Holiday singing 'Gloomy Sunday'. She must have had other records, even if only briefly: she danced the tango with one of her men and there was certainly music then, but the only record I can remember is the Billie Holiday. That strange, dragging vocal line, the voice harsh, almost discordant at times, grit mixed with honey; flexible, warm, seductive, singing a hymn to suicide.

The child is three and they are on their way to a hill station to escape the heat of the plains, taking the train, rocked to sleep, waking in the night to see empty fields lit by the moon, the platforms of small stations carpeted with sleeping forms, white-shrouded, stiff and straight as corpses.

At dawn there are buffaloes by a river, unmoving, like lumps of dark, wet mud; on their backs, small white birds hop busily. The ayah tells her the birds live by seeking out and consuming the vermin on the buffalo.

9

The beasts seem unaware of the beaks pecking at their skin.

The hill station is called Naini Tal and overlooks a lake. The ayah says it is bottomless, that from its depths demons pull unwise bathers beneath the surface, and one day they see a body carried ashore – an Englishman – swollen and limp. The ayah nods, pursing her lips, unsurprised.

I walked down the Naini hillside through sunflowers that grew taller than my head. They were a grove of saplings to me, the tough, fuzzy stalks, the huge yellow heads open above my head, turned to the prevailing sun; there was the buzz of bees visiting the flowers, a sharp, lemony smell. It was after that we went home. Or rather, returned to one of the places called by that name.

Trains and rivers were always part of it: trains and rivers running side by side, crossing each other. We moved along ancient routes, the Ganges, the Jumna, the Hooghly sacred rivers, sacred both at the source and the junctions, each feeding the next. The trains too, fed from each other, city to city, across a landscape of dry, dust-coloured fields and velvet, creamy bullocks; of sun so fierce that even the shadows beneath the trees glowed with light.

The train smelled of soot. The black, shiny, slightly scratchy stuff of the seats grew hot and sticky beneath my bare legs; the big block of ice in sawdust, melting slowly into the square zinc tub in the middle of the compartment floor, rocked and slopped like a choppy sea.

Whole days in the train. Lunch at station dining rooms; soot from the engine stinging the eyes at open windows. The sound of the train at night, suddenly loud, clattering over high wooden bridges, rattling past dark stations, the platforms white with those ghostly sleeping forms.

My father met us at the station.

'Good trip?'

'Mm. Yes.'

They kissed, perfunctorily. He ruffled my hair. We climbed into the Lagonda. Was it a Lagonda? She always said so, later, but it might have been just a Ford. She had a way of colouring the past that makes me mistrust my own memories. Did it happen? Did she tell me it happened? Does it matter which?

Life at home was unchanged: I rode my pony, encircled by the leather ring saddle which held me safe. The dancing class was on Tuesday and Thursday.

We were preparing a show for the club; it would be charming, Miss Austell promised. She organized the details: 'A wooden floor, sprung, laid out on the lawn, isn't that lovely?'

It was to be 'The Wedding of the Painted Doll': an extravaganza with costumes, scenery – potted palms placed round the wooden floor – music . . .

The children were thrilled with their costumes; fairies in sweet-pea colours of gauze and tulle; dolls with red cheeks and button boots, sailor boys. Frogs.

The club was a square white building, its dusty compound set about with tamarind trees, but round the back it became England: green lawns, flower beds, fruit trees. The lawn sloped slightly to provide a natural theatrical hollow and the committee had set out spindly chairs in curving rows. Wives looked their prettiest, the men were heroic, concealing boredom and impatience.

A gramophone provided the music. The unavoidable pause when the 78 record needed turning over; the barely perceptible wavering of the tempo and pitch as

11

the handle was vigorously turned, only added to the excitement. And the children were good. The applause at the end was genuine. Except from my mother, from Moti.

'Yes, Moti,' she would say, laughing, 'blame the child, she started it.' Did I? When I first began to speak (here again I have to rely on what I am told) I tried, it seems, to say 'Mother' but what came out was 'moti'. The ayah was much amused, *moti* being Hindi for pearl. The servants' quarters were informed, so were my mother's friends, and the name stuck. Not at the club, of course, where she remained Diana, but among her other friends, the ones she met in town. There she became Moti, the pearl of the cocktail set.

I myself never used the name once I had outgrown the original, innocent mangling. Soon I outgrew other forms of address too, and in time became incapable of calling my mother by any name at all.

In the club garden, Moti stands, stony faced, and watches 'The Wedding of the Painted Doll'. The gramophone churns out the song; the children prance and twirl as the sky turns pale yellow and a flock of small birds swoops low overhead. The wooden dance floor has crushed the lawn and with the lengthening shadows the earth releases a smell of damp grass, cool as a long drink.

Afterwards, when the curtsies and bows are over, when the other children cluster round parents and friends noisily anatomizing the performance, Moti waits, one long finger tapping the back of a gilded chair as a small figure hops towards her.

'You didn't tell me you were to be a frog.'

She has leaped splendidly, her small body and sturdy legs clad in bright green material. Miss Austell has praised her elevation, her *ballon*. ('Not quite four, and

12

such control!') She hops on the spot. 'Croak!' she says loudly, nodding her frog head-dress decorated with pop eyes and a wide-mouthed grin.

'You didn't tell me you were a frog,' Moti repeats.

The child looks up, the round face absurd beneath the frog-grin. 'It was a secret. A surprise.'

'It certainly was.'

The dancing teacher approaches, radiant, unsuspecting, and Moti turns on her murderously.

'I do not pay for dancing lessons to be made a fool of. I do not find it amusing to see my daughter humiliated. She will not be attending classes in future.'

Miss Austell gapes, stunned by the outburst. The child, gazing up at her mother, takes in the white face, the furious eyes, and her smile slips.

'I *liked* being a frog –'

Moti turns and walks away across the lawn, her high heels spiking the turf. Miss Austell's eyes are filled with tears. She is a plain, earnest woman with a broad face, like a moon, and a way of bending forward encouragingly when addressing parents. The child looks at her feet, blinking rapidly. Miss Austell sees only the top of her head, the grinning frog, the pop eyes. 'You didn't tell me you were unhappy as a frog. You should have told me.' She walks away.

A small event, but it played its part in a larger scheme. Moti boycotted the post-performance celebration at the club. She ordered the car and drove into town. I was taken home and left with the servants.

Faintly through the trees came the sound of voices, laughter, music. An entertainer had been engaged, a magician, to produce rabbits and a flaming cake from a top hat, to wave coloured handkerchiefs and draw eggs from ears and nostrils. Very English magic, transplanted from the Home Counties. Harmless. Circumscribed.

13

A pity, missing the party, but magic was not confined to the club. It was all around us. Sitting with the servants in the compound I listened to stories of ghosts and demons, of monkeys that assumed human form and humans terribly changed by spells.

It grows dark and the lamp throws the shadow of the tamarind tree against the compound wall. On one branch a monkey squats, bouncing and chattering. The tree, the monkey, the lamplight are real enough, ordinary. But the shadow is somehow different: as the monkey bounces more vigorously, the shadow looms huge and menacing, then shrinks only to spring out again like a genie from a bottle. In the warm, scented air the child sits hugging her knees, the frog dance forgotten, the murmuring of the servants' voices in the background, a rapture of fear gripping her as she stares at the monstrously swelling and shrinking shadow on the compound wall.

She listens to their stories. Mysterious, magical events are always taking place – 'It happened, I tell you this really happened, in my sister's husband's village there was a man who could . . .', 'a woman who knew . . .'

Her mother refuses to allow the servants to speak English to the child – 'We don't want a singsong Anglo accent, do we?' – so she speaks Hindi to them, learning it easily, naturally, as her father had, at ease with the language and the people. Moti has never bothered to learn anything beyond pidgin-level: 'Fetch, take, quickly . . . yes, no, too much chilli . . . whisky soda, *burra peg* . . .'

There is a new houseboy, Saiid, he is telling the ayah he does not intend to remain a servant, he would like to be a dancer.

'How old are you?' the woman demands.

'Fifteen.'

'Go back to your family.' She sounds disapproving. This is strange: surely to be a dancer is a good thing? Moti talks of dancing, of ballet-dancing anyway, as a vocation. The ayah moves away a few yards, settling near one of the older servants, her voice falling into a blurred mutter. The child stops listening.

I was christened Margaret-Rose after the little princess, and when introducing me to people my mother used the full, hyphenated name: 'This is Margaret-Rose. Margaret-Rose wants to be a ballet-dancer. We talked to Alicia Markova about it once and she advised . . .' Well, perhaps she did.

Alone together, she called me Maggie. 'Oh Maggie, my head hurts, the pain is bad today . . .' and the pale, bony face would be lowered, the eyelids fluttering, blue veins lacing white skin, so that I could rub gently, insistently, as the ayah had shown me, massaging the pain away.

But when her mother is with her friends, or with some particular friend (Maggie notices that she likes sometimes to have long conversations with people not of the club crowd; these are usually men. Their conversations are mysterious, half-heard, puzzling, punctuated by explosions of quickly suppressed laughter, sometimes ending in silences, abrupt departures), at these times her mother calls her the Child. 'The Child has to be taken home, it's past her bedtime.'

Thus, later, she hears Moti recount the story of the club entertainment. '. . . No sign of her among the fairies or the dolls. I thought: she's been given a solo spot – the child can dance you know – and then, there she is, hopping onto the stage, bright green, got up as a bloody frog. I ask you. I mean, she's no beauty, but – a frog! I know what's behind it, of course.'

What? she wants to ask. What? So often it is like this:

15

it away with a small, flimsy handkerchief. They are together in a cool, dim paradise that smells of fresh cream and where there are no raised voices, no mysteries.

My father never went to the ABC dairy. It would have struck him as foolish and probably bad form.

'You think like a bloody Indian!' Moti snapped at him once, her voice hard and loud.

'Thank you,' he said pleasantly.

He liked blazing hot curries which he consumed very quickly, sweating, and making small puffing and blowing noises which Moti found unbearable.

'Must you?'

'It's hot.'

'Too much chilli –'

'It's how I like it.'

She shrugged. Her mouth curled. 'Of course.'

He was a quiet man, stocky and sallow, with heavy shoulders which gave him the air of stooping slightly. He was the same height as his wife, but his hunched shoulders and her extravagantly high heels gave her an extra three inches when they went out together. She sometimes gave the impression she was looking over the top of his head.

They met one summer when he spent a long leave in England. Someone introduced them at a party; he heard she was going back to Dundee the next day and reserved a seat in the same compartment. He was twenty-nine, ten years older than she was. Everyone knew that a long leave for a twenty-nine-year-old bachelor could mean only one thing: he was in search of a bride.

They all said he was the wrong man for her: Diana's father (the 'eminent architect' as she so often referred to him, the professional Scot, a man of disappointed ambitions) mistrusted him.

18

'I do not care for the way he looks at her with those lascivious brown eyes.'

Diana, who had thought of her suitor as rather dull, found him suddenly of more interest. Lascivious brown eyes? She looked it up: *'Inclined to lust; lewd; voluptuous.'*

Well.

There was nothing her father could have said better calculated to send her hastening into the young man's arms. He had a hard body, breath untainted by tobacco, and his teeth were white, large and regular.

When he smiled, the action creating deep creases in cheeks already leathery from the sun, she read into the ambiguity of the smile all sorts of intriguing possibilities. She knew nothing and hoped excessively. They were married before the season was out.

Some of this she told me, or I overheard her telling friends, smiling bitterly, dwelling on the fatal adjective 'lascivious'. I gleaned a word here, an indication there, picking up clues.

A sea voyage was not the place to discover the truth about someone, but there were things Moti did learn: that he disliked dancing, saw no point in it. That 'chatter' was alien to him. That he was capable of silence beyond her comprehension. Gradually she saw that he was a man for whom quiet was important, even vital. And in whose brown eyes she had perhaps seen more than was justified. But by then she was settled into Amaryllis with its dusty red compound and its shaggy tamarind tree. And she was pregnant.

So the houseboy wanted to be a dancer. I saw that this was evidently not the same thing as wanting to follow in the *pointes* of Alicia Markova.

'Margaret-Rose wants to be a ballet-dancer.' I never did want to be a ballet-dancer. An acrobat, possibly: I was supple as a mongoose; I did cartwheels, and walked on my hands. I could leap and spin with great flair. But I was more concerned with the testing of the muscles than the tutu. It was she who wanted Margaret-Rose to be a ballet-dancer.

I had seen Indian dancers erupt into the street at festival times: tall, beautiful, with nose jewels, their heavily kohl-ringed eyes flashing, anklets chinking as they stamped and twirled, skirts flaring, supple fingers telling the story of the dance. There were mysteries here too: these dancers were not, it seemed, quite what they appeared to be. The smiles that greeted their mock-provocative hip-thrusts were knowing. It was not for the ayah to tell me they were men, transvestites, as I discovered later, but she clearly felt herself a cut above such people. So when the houseboy talked of dancing, she moved away, leaving him solitary, to stare at the shadows leaping on the compound wall, and waggle his head sideways in tiny rhythmic movements, in time to music unheard by the rest.

She is nearly four – far too old for the drop-side cot, but it is large and she is small, so she sleeps in it still, climbing in, pulling up the sides like a drawbridge.

Not yet asleep, watching the glow the nightlight casts on the white wall, Maggie becomes aware that someone has come into the room. Not the ayah, who is probably asleep in the corridor. It is Saiid, the houseboy. He smiles and waves, giggling silently. She watches him through the bars, sitting up, pressing her cheeks against the rounded strips of wood.

His hands are speaking, fingers eloquent: watch now, you will see something amusing . . . extraordinary . . .

He stands on the spot, moving his body, thrusting his hips back and forth, grinding them in circular movements. His loose cotton trousers are tented comically in front of him: something – a snake? a magic stick? – is trying to thrust its way out. He grins and waggles his head. She laughs. He does not seem to be a very good dancer.

The child sees Moti first: Moti, home early from the club, stepping into the room, smiling, then taking in the houseboy, and what he is doing. Her arm comes up fast and she swings it, open-palmed, striking him hard across the head. Knocked off balance he hits the marble floor, screaming with surprise and pain. The ayah rushes in. There are shrieks. The child begins to cry.

The dance had seemed funny. Her mother's intervention has turned it into something frightening. Was there something to be afraid of? Not the houseboy, surely? He was showing off, but so did they all, at dancing class.

He scrambles to his feet, runs for the door. Her mother pursues him, shouting abuse. She grabs a plate, sends it skimming at his head. Sprinting for the gate he looks back, sees the china discus homing in and instinctively flings up a hand to catch it without slackening pace. He disappears down the road in a cloud of dust, pale in the darkness. Her mother's face is white. This country, she keeps muttering. This bloody country. These people.

A few days later the houseboy is seen hanging about outside the gate. By next day he has ventured into the compound. Moti stands on the veranda, he at the bottom of the steps. He reaches into his jacket and brings out the plate she hurled at his head.

'It is part of a set,' he explains in Hindi. 'I was sure the Memsahib would like it returned. Such a pretty plate. Valuable.'

She signals to a servant to take the plate. He beams hopefully. 'Can I have my job back?' She knows enough to understand him.

'He frightened my daughter. I cannot trust him.'

The message is passed on to him. For a moment he

21

stands motionless, then he turns away, towards the gate. He is almost there when he begins to shout: his mother is sick. They need the money. His brother is dying; there is a man who could save him, a man with great powers, magic. But healing is expensive. He needs the work –

The gatekeeper hustles him out of sight, out onto the road. The red-brown dust settles. The child walks down the veranda steps to the sand-pit beneath the tamarind tree.

It was always dusty in town. Noisy with wheels and the shouts of men urging on overloaded, underfed horses and donkeys; with people buying, selling, locked in endless argument. Home was quiet, except for those nights when I woke to the sound of English voices: of my mother's, hard, angry, jagged; of his, tired, muted at first, then loud with bitterness.

In the morning, blinds of woven grass were lowered over the east-facing windows and veranda, and sprayed with water. All day there was a smell of wet matting drying out in the heat of the sun, the squeak of the overhead fans turning, the feel of the chip marble underfoot, smooth and cool at first, later growing warm and sticky. I often went barefoot and in time the soles of my feet hardened and calloused so that, like the servants, I could walk out in the burning compound without flinching. Moti worried that I might 'pick up something', but I knew that even were I to do so, somewhere there would be a man with strange, magical powers who would cure it.

Malaria takes over her body and she lies shivering and sweating in turns, teeth chattering, bones aching, the ceiling swinging above her like earthquake time. Quinine is bitter in her mouth. Will she die, like those pavement dwellers who are discovered stiff and cold in the morning, who have not survived the night? Will she be burned at the ghats?

Sickness, deformity and magic were all around us. The sickness of the beggars, largely disregarded; the lepers, fingers and features dissolving; the legless, the blind, the suppurating. Flies clustered thick on their sore-infested heads like glistening black coronets. The man with elephantiasis, dragging his hugely enlarged leg around like a tree-trunk. I heard the servants discussing a man similarly afflicted, but in the testicles, so that he pushed a sort of trolley about before him, to hold the swollen organs, rather like the Dumba fat-tailed sheep I had seen in the hills, each with a little cart attached to carry its enormous, and later succulent, tail.

Disease must be kept at bay: I have a big, deeply-pocked vaccination mark on my thigh. When it was done I spent two blazing, feverish weeks in my cot with a leg like hot, hard rubber while the vaccination puffed and darkened with inflammation until it looked like a waffle. Moti scorned vaccination for herself; she disliked the idea of scars on her flesh, and besides, vaccination was all part of bloody India.

The child is the centre of a cone of silence, a blanked-out un-noise roaring in her ears. The silence follows the shouting: English voices raised, threats offered. In another room they are fighting.

A glass bell descends, shutting out all noise. Inside the bell movement is slowed down. She watches herself speaking, turning, reaching out, but the rushing silence slows it all, like movements made under water.

She goes swimming with her mother at the club. Water wings, energetic frog-kicks, splashing. Fun. Then she sits on the edge while Moti swims steadily up and down the pool, breast-stroke, side-stroke, back-stroke, up and down. She pauses for breath, holding the child's feet, her face blue-white against the green swimming cap.

'One day,' she says, 'I shall dive to the bottom of the pool and stay there. Forever.' She shakes water out of her eyes. 'Goodbye,' she calls and shoots away from the side, raising her arm in a slow, farewell wave. She heads for the centre of the pool and is gone, in a swirl of ripples and a bubbling wake.

Maggie watches the bubbles and waits, confidently, for her surfacing head to come into view. The moments pass. No sign. The surface steadies. The pool is empty. She runs along the edge, searching, and begins to cry, to call for help. People come running. Then her mother surfaces, laughing.

*   *   *

We were going home, Moti said, on a visit. But surely this was home. Here was another mystery, but as on so many occasions, it was difficult to get answers to questions. Moti was bored by the riots, or so she said. As though in explanation.

'These people,' she said. She had opinions: they fought among themselves, they always had, she said, they always would. She who knew nothing of their history, who could barely speak their language, was bored by them. So riots did not normally bother her; she regarded them as native matters and calculated, correctly, that if she paid no attention to them she would in turn be left alone. She also voiced the opinion that if they were ignored they would fizzle out, and here she proved less accurate, though she would not realize that for some time.

Perhaps the latest disturbances were more difficult to ignore: more concentrated, lasting longer than usual.

24

Fires blazed; the sound of the mob was closer. Wives and children, it was decided, would sleep inside the mill, just in case. That night, quickly but discreetly, wicket gates leading from bungalow compounds into mill grounds were unlocked, women and children bundled through. I wore a night-dress and riding boots to protect my feet. It became an excursion. The mill smelled pungently of wool and machine oil. The deserted mill within its high wall was foreign territory; the children were noisy, over-excited, and there were tears before camp-bed time.

It seemed a convenient time to go home on a visit, and at Amaryllis things had in any case been going badly. There was the episode of the dancing bear.

Moti had bought a dancing bear she saw being ill-treated in the street by its owner. She thought to give it to the local zoo but they declined: dancing bears bought in the bazaar were not, it seemed, ideal zoo material. She must place it elsewhere. This would surely be a simple matter, but in the meantime there was a crocodile shoot down river, an invitation from the Maharaja. Rude to let him down. The servants declared that caring for a dancing bear was outside the scope of their duties. She pointed out that it was a thoroughly tame bear. A docile bear. A pet, really. The chain between its feet clanked sadly when it moved. It was about eight feet tall.

'The poor lamb,' Moti said, and planned to leave it loose, but the servants proved so unimpressed by this idea that she agreed, reluctantly, to chain the animal up to something solid, just to reassure the staff.

The *mali* found a thick cornerpost off an outhouse and drove it deep into the ground. The bear's chain was attached to the post. He looked dejected, sleepy. The shaggy dark fur was matted and dusty; his nostrils and eyes looked sore beneath a coat of dust.

Moti gave a cocktail party that evening, before leaving for the croc hunt, and guests wandered up to the bear, slumped at the end of the garden, tethered to his post. They stared at him, surprised, and the bear raised a heavy head and looked at them dully with small, rust-coloured eyes. They found him of limited interest, though one or two of the women fed him canapés and one of the men poured a gin into his dish to cheer him up.

Around breakfast time next morning the bear rose to his feet, shook himself briskly, tore the stake out of the ground and began to demolish the garden.

From my bedroom window I watched him, surprisingly fast on his feet now and not much impeded by the chain. The roaring and crashing brought the servants running, but what was to be done? The Memsahib was off on her crocodile shoot; the Sahib was already at the mill. Meanwhile the bear was on the rampage: dragging the heavy beam behind him, he tore up flower beds, tasting the bright orange blooms and spitting them out; he smashed fences and trampled lawn to dust. His paws, the servants noted aloud, were equipped with extremely large claws; he had teeth, his jaws were wide, his eyes, no longer sleepy, glittered dark red.

A message was despatched to the mill: 'The beast is destroying the garden . . .' My father called the vet, who seemed to find the entire story unbelievable. Buying a *bear*? . . . putting it in the *garden*? . . . Well it seemed so docile, we offered in extenuation.

He frowned impatiently. 'Sedated, of course. They always are. Should have thought you'd know that.'

The bear was out of control, one paw bleeding, a public danger if he escaped from the garden. He would have to be destroyed. It was an unfortunate business. Father took the vet to the club for a stiff drink; invited him back to dinner with Miss Austell, the dancing teacher. I stayed up for lemonade and peanuts while they sat over their pre-dinner drinks. The two men talked, the woman listened, turning her moon-face from one to the other like a watcher at a club tennis match. It was a quiet evening, not many laughs, and afterwards they listened to Beethoven on the radiogram. Nobody mentioned the bear.

At Amaryllis, when Moti got back, the mood was bleak: she thought he had been unsympathetic; he thought she had been idiotic. A good time for a voyage, yes. For this trip 'home', on a visit.

We drove to the railway station very early in the morning. The sky was still grey, then slowly the enormous crimson ball of the sun bulged over the horizon and rested for a moment, heavy. A few seconds later it had shed its weight and, bled of its dark colour, it bounded clear of the earth's curve, turning to fiery gold. In an hour's time it would already be at full heat: a disc, thin, like beaten silver, rendering the scene below it colourless, bleached out by that harsh, comfortless glare.

(When we reached England I realized for the first time what the Bengal sun did to people. I saw that I had sallow skin, quite different from the rosy, tanned glow of the cousins I met in Scotland, the pink-and-white children encountered in Hyde Park with their nannies. My skin was yellow tinged, drained of life by that punishing sun.)

At the station her father says goodbye. He hugs her briefly, picking her up, cradling her in his long arms. He looks at her. In the distorting mirror of his face she sees her own, enlarged, creased, grown rough. The same round brown eyes, the same blob of nose, the same wide mouth, ambiguous smile. He nods at her, rubs noses, and puts her down.

She looks up at the two of them towering above her, he in shorts and short-sleeved shirt, Moti in pale frock and white gloves, silk stockings of a whitish tinge. He slaps the side of his shorts absently with one hand, as though brushing off dust. Her mother's eyes flicker: she is irritated by the mannerism. She finds it hard to be close to him. When the prickly heat rash spreads across his thighs and body in the hot weather she makes sure there is plenty of boracic lint in the medical cupboard and drives off into town in search of a cooling drink.

He had seemed exotic, almost foreign, when she first saw him, tanned and brown against the greyness of Scottish granite. Here he was all too ordinary: a bleached-out man in a bleached-out landscape. Even his seriousness was a handicap. She loved to laugh, to joke and tease and outrage. He found quick and easy laughter an unsatisfactory antidote to darkness. There seemed no common ground.

He sought for words. 'The change will do you good.'
'Mm.'
'Write, won't you?'
'Oh yes. And you.'

In my experience her letters are rare as unicorns, even a message a chore too great to be committed to paper, time too short to be spent scribbling it. She might as well have lived before the invention of writing: communication for her was physical or non-existent.

Years later, a kind man – one of her many kind men – bought a present for my birthday: a leather-bound bible with coloured illustrations. He wrote his name on the flyleaf and left Moti to fill in hers, along with a maternal line of greeting and affection, before wrapping it.

He had intended it to read, *'With love from Mummy and Shorty'*, but he had reckoned without her vast inertia, her ability to overlook. On my birthday I opened the gold-edged leather cover to find the cryptic words, *'and Shorty'*.

Astonishingly the book has survived sea crossings, sudden departures, bombs, neglect and a second generation of childish fingers. I have it still. Shorty went his way soon after writing that inscription. He cried, as they sometimes did. But the bible stayed. And message: *'and Shorty'*.

But that was all much later.

The train to Bombay, the dock, the boat. How Moti enjoyed that crossing! It had the virtue of parenthesis: all connection, all responsibility severed for this space of time. She was free to enjoy herself without guilt or caution. The band played every day. She danced the rumba, the foxtrot, the tango. She did more than merely enjoy, she created conviviality, animation; she was sharp as a flint-head, striking laughter and response from those around her.

After those last few, listless weeks at Amaryllis she seemed suddenly twice as alive: when she raised her smooth head to meet the glance of an interesting new acquaintance, her eyes snapped wide, her neck lengthened like a swan's. She moved on the dance floor as though skating on ice, cutting through the crowd, elegantly sharp, sure of herself.

There was one particular dancing partner who quickly established a claim: a tea-planter going home on leave. Alexander was tall, nearly six foot, with a flawless profile and a penchant for white tie and tails.

Alexander was unusual: he paid attention not only to Moti, but to me, squatting down, disregarding damage to superb white flannels to converse eye to eye, listen, nod, question. Like Moti, he was Scottish, but unlike her he had not lost his brogue.

'Well now, Maggie, can you not read yet? Six words by tomorrow, mind.'

He is a prince, a knight. Maggie wishes the crossing would take not three weeks but forever. He tells her stories, fills her head with images of fabulous beasts from the lochs and heathery mountains. His voice sings the words, lifting them, reshaping them strangely, making them magical.

He studies the pasteboard pages of her reading book with her while Moti is at the hairdresser or resting below.

'Do you not see, Maggie, you must build up the words, with pieces like bricks . . .'

The crossing would be perfection but for the man with the teeth. Maggie notices him a few days out, and the next day he offers her a biscuit when they meet one morning on the deserted, windy side of the deck.

'No, thank you.'

One thing Moti has instilled into the child is that you do not accept sweets or presents from strangers. Nor do you agree to go for little walks with them – not even round the deck. She flees, almost tripping over, and looking back she sees him smiling after her. He is a thin man whose clothes hang loosely on him; balding, he has pale eyes and skin that seems stretched over the bones of his face. His teeth are yellowish but very regular, and when he smiles his lips retract so that the teeth and the gums seem to grow, filling his face to crowd out his other features. The teeth pursue her as she runs.

She sees him several times in the next few days, usually in the distance, but once, too late to avoid him, she finds him at the top of a flight of stairs, staring down at her as she climbs towards the deck.

As she comes level with him she sees that he carries something in his hands: a pink, rubber tube like a sloughed snakeskin. He pulls at it without haste, stretching the rubbery stuff, elongating it till it thins and pales, then releasing it to snap back into his palm, quivering pinkly. His movements are hypnotic, the stretching and shrinking – like the monkey's shadow on the compound wall – menacing, frightening. Her mouth dry, she edges past him, out onto the deck.

They have crossed the equator. Maggie is unsure what this is: a line running round the earth? But where? If far below them on the ocean floor, how did they know it was there at all? And if on the surface, how could they 'cross' it without cutting it or being held back? Did ships float over this line or was it hanging above them in the sky? Once, she began to put some of these questions, but grown-up, amused glances silenced her. She hates the indulgent smiles, hates those who crease their faces and twinkle at her kindly. Suddenly filled with super-human strength she hurls them effortlessly from the deck, over the rail, watches them flailing as they vanish into the dark, foaming water while the ship throbs on steadily. If only she could. Instead she stares up at them, eyes flat, face expressionless.

Moti told people later, 'Margaret-Rose could read at three – I found her reading *Gulliver's Travels* one day when she was barely four . . .'

The pictures were wonderful: magical beasts, things freed from their normal size, their everyday relationship. But did I really read it at four? Mother said so. Memory processes the data and here I am, reading Gulliver at four.

*

Maggie is looking at a book called *Gulliver's Travels*. The pictures are nice. Frightening, but warm-frightening; burrowing down, shivering into bedclothes frightening, not cold, slithery, skull-and-yellow-teeth frightening.

On the day before they are due into Southampton she walks round the deck. It is cold; she breathes out gustily, white breath fuelling the mist.

The greyness settles on her face like wet cobwebs. Her lashes stick together, tangled spiders' legs. When she opens her eyes, the man with yellow teeth is standing braced against one of the heavy iron doors off the deck. She could walk on, round the curve of the bow, but it is cold, windy, and he might follow. And anyway, what is there to be afraid of? He has done nothing. She will simply not look at him.

She pauses by the iron door, climbing carefully over the jutting iron threshold. Off balance, one foot still in the air, she makes the mistake of glancing up, past buttons, collar, tie, to his face, to the drawn-back lips, the smile, the teeth.

In a movement so swift she misses it, his hands flash up to his mouth and the teeth come away in his hands as though wrenched out entire from his jaw. He thrusts them at her, a double horror: the grinning yellow teeth and waxy gums, swooping, wetly, inches from her nose. Above them, his toothless grin, lips drawn back over black emptiness. He is laughing silently.

For a moment shock paralyses movement, kills sound in her throat. Then she begins to scream and scream.

Tripping as she tries to run, falling, getting up, falling again, she screams into a black blindness. Someone picks her up; she fights, gasping, eyes shut tight, still screaming. Voices, hands, the feet of many people pressing round her, dispelling the terror, soothing.

From somewhere, Moti appears, stroking, murmuring useless reassurances. No one can understand what has caused the trouble.

'I'm afraid the child is highly strung,' Moti says.

I never told her about the man with the teeth.

She, on the other hand, liked to pass things on, to talk in the bath, stretched out like a Bonnard nude, with me sitting on the floor, stroking the soft material of her high-heeled mules. The bath water was greenish, resisting lather. Her skin gleamed pale through the brackish water. I squeezed the sponge and the water ran down her shoulders, her raised arms. At home there were no sponges: scorpions could crawl into the holes of a dry sponge as they sometimes found their way into shoes and slippers. So a sponge was something new, a plaything. I dunked and squeezed.

'Sometimes,' she said, 'I think it might be nice to live alone. I don't mean away from *you*, of course. But . . .' She rubbed her body dreamily. 'I suffered a lot, having you. I nearly died, they said. I went through hell.' I knew all this: my beginning almost causing her ending was familiar through repetition.

'But if it were just the two of us . . . we'd have fun, wouldn't we?'

'Yes,' I said obediently.

I knew her surfaces, I watched her paint her toe-nails scarlet, shave her armpits. The little razor glittered as she stroked and stroked, slicing away the hairs, attacking the dark stubble until the skin grew as smooth and white as her breasts.

She hid no physical aspect of herself. But when she left the room she ceased to exist – I had no means of learning more. Her actions were all I had to know her by.

'To be with someone morning, noon and night,' she

33

said, 'it can be too much.' But she was not with him all that often.

He rose at five, breakfasted at six and was the other side of the wicket gate before she woke. She rarely ate lunch; he consumed his blazing curries quickly, punctuated by those little puffing noises, cooling his mouth with draughts of beer.

At the club he played billiards or squash, she moved from group to group, hearing music from the next room, longing to dance, occasionally enjoying a joke – 'glad to see *someone* who's not totally desiccated by this bloody climate', someone who could rise to the demands of frivolity.

How do I know this? This cannot be my memory, throwing up these images; I cannot have actually seen those evenings of nervy, claustrophobic boredom. She gave me a present of it all, later, endlessly repeated, variations on a theme.

My father listened to Beethoven on his radiogram. He had a recording of the Kreutzer Sonata with George Kulenkampff, which did not impress Moti who claimed to have met the violinist at some grand affair in Berlin before she was married. 'It's not the Kreutzer Sonata, anyway – it's really the Sonata Mulattica: Beethoven wrote it for some nigger friend of his who played the violin.'

She said all this as though somehow it made it unnecessary for her now to listen to this so-called Kreutzer.

He knew she was making it up – she did so all the time – and it irritated him when he discovered later that it happened to be true. This was one of her tricks: every now and then, into the cat's cradle of fantasy and lies she dropped unlikely statements, nuggets of improbable knowledge which were genuine. She refused to be categorized. She flowed, shapeless as water through

34

our lives, taking this form or that, now sparkling, now stagnant, dangerous.

'Sonata Mulattica,' she said contemptuously, leaving the room with that haughty tilt of the head, the greenish eyes, like a Siamese cat's, seeming to squint slightly as she looked down her long, thin nose, the nostrils pinched.

Decades later I heard another Kreutzer Sonata – Janáček's – and with wonderment recognized my mother in the music: the authentic neurasthenic, edgy note, like nails screeching on slate; the abrupt see-saw between high spirits and something darker that encroached like sudden shadow on a sunlit field of corn.

We were booked into the Charing Cross Hotel. A paradise: a hotel surrounded by trains – the smell and sound of trains, the clanking of pistons, the slow wheeze of engines getting up steam, the bustle from the platforms, the reception hall full of people with luggage, porters, a sense of arrivals and departures.

'It's only for a night or two, until we get organized,' Moti said, and lay down to rest.

I explored the hotel: the wide staircase with glass-smooth balustrade; the chandeliers, the fluted columns, the lifts gliding up and down. The long, dimly lit corridors, thickly carpeted, labyrinthine . . .

The corridor is very long; it intersects with another. They all look the same. She realizes she is lost. At the far end there is a flicker of movement. She stops, uncertain, and waits, but no one comes. She moves on again, and again she sees it: the flutter far down the corridor. She walks on, determined to conquer nervousness, and is rewarded: walking towards her is a girl, her size! There will be someone to talk to, a friend. Eagerly she begins to run to meet the stranger, who, as eagerly, comes towards her. Closer, closer, she can see her smiling –

The impact is shattering: not to the vast mirror which covers the entire wall at the end of the corridor, but to the child who has run full tilt into it.

Stunned, knocked senseless, a huge bump already rising on her forehead, she is found by a chambermaid, picked up and carried back to her mother.

Moti puts her to bed, smiling, irritated. First hysteria on the ship, now this . . . 'Maybe she's short-sighted,' the chambermaid suggests. 'Maybe she needs glasses.' Moti stops smiling.

'Oh no, I think not.' *Glasses?* With a tutu? 'The corridor is rather dark. Better lighting is certainly needed. I shall speak to the manager.'

But in any case they are leaving the Charing Cross Hotel: Alexander is organizing their lives.

London, I discovered, was like an ocean liner with longer walks. The hotel room, the waiters serving meals, the dance band, the public rooms filled with well-dressed people, it all seemed very P & O. But the park, the statue of Peter Pan, the buses and taxis were new and astonishing. No horse-drawn carriages smelling of hot leather and dung; no men running barefoot and sweating between the shafts of rickshaws, no Indians. White faces filled the streets, pale as unbaked dough. The absence of brown skin seemed odd. I had not realized 'home' would not include Indians.

Alexander took us to restaurants, bundling us into taxis, taking care of the details. He took us for drives in the country (was it really a Bentley with a leather strap over the bonnet? Later Moti always said so.) When he took her dancing, or to dinner, she wore long, slithery frocks with nothing underneath.

36

'I should never have breast-fed the Child . . .' She looked at herself in the pink mirror. 'There's nothing left.' And knickers were apparently hopeless under slim skirts, showing up in ridges, 'very ugly'.

Knickers were a problem generally. On one occasion, crossing Piccadilly Circus, Moti stopped, glancing down without concern as her silk French knickers dropped to her ankles. 'Blast,' she said, 'the bloody button's come off.'

My eyes were level with her knees. The thin, silky knickers lay in a pale coffee pool at her feet. Taxis hooted, cars veered as we stood in mid-stream, disrupting the traffic. Calmly she stepped out of the ring of silk, picked up the knickers and dropped them into her large crocodile handbag. The chunky silver clasp snapped shut with a click.

'Come along,' she said impatiently, 'we'll be late for lunch.'

Later, bored with the unpredictability of underwear, and disinclined to waste time washing it herself when servants were no longer available, she often discarded it altogether.

Alexander took her to the opera. There is a photograph of the two of them, he in tails, she swathed in fur, though who took it, and why, remains a mystery. There was another mystery; another photograph, taken at the same time, the surface matt and slightly stippled, the tone almost sepia in its softness. It is a picture of mother and child.

I am four, wearing a tutu. (*Why?* For dance classes I wore leotards; she must have got me up for the picture, another of her fantasies – I am already on the way to a début.) 'Margaret-Rose is training to be a ballet-dancer.

Luckily she's small, you can't have a *tall* soloist. Yes, she's really rather good, we've come home to find her a better teacher . . .'

(We had come home to get her away from Beethoven and the club. Away from Amaryllis. A good dancing teacher was low on the list of priorities.)

So: I am four, in a tutu. My hair in the picture is curly, bouncy with curls like a cherub. For once I look like the Shirley Temple child she desires.

She is in evening dress. A long, slim column of heavy midnight-blue silk, bias-cut, her shoulders bare, the halter-neck of the dress drawn up by a thick, crunchy rope of gold silk which hangs down her spine. Her back bare to the waist, she looks particularly naked in this dress, the heavy, dark blue fabric and thick gold silk rope dark against her smooth, very white flesh.

Her hair is brushed smooth and coiled on her nape. She wears ear-rings – sapphires? Alexander gave her sapphires – and fragile, high-heeled dark sandals.

I have an awareness of Alexander just out of frame, waiting to sweep her off to Glyndebourne or Covent Garden. I can smell 'Ma Griffe'.

How rich we are in the photograph! The spindly walnut table in the background has a silver cigarette box on it; silk curtains hang at the windows. She has picked me up, careless of shoes against delicate fabric (though they are of course only satin ballet slippers), and links her arms round my buttocks. My legs entwined round her, my arms on her shoulders, we look at one another. Her face is serene, her mouth relaxed in a curve of satisfaction. Her long face bends towards mine, benign.

And the child's face – round eyes above cheeks curved like apples – is raised to hers, uncritical, admiring. It is a moment of mutual adoration, madonna and child,

38

grave, each wrapped – rapt? – in contemplation of the other.

Beyond the frame a man coughs. The woman frees herself, leaves the room, the photograph and the child.

Thrown over her shoulder there is a fur, silver fox. The door closes, the child is alone. The hotel room becomes larger, its pink and apricot hues cold. There will be hours of emptiness. Slowly she begins to unlace the ribbons of the ballet shoes.

A little later that evening, one of the hotel guests sees a child standing by the door of the Powder Room: she looks alert, composed, at ease.

'Do forgive me, but I wonder if you could possibly pull the chain for me? I can't quite reach, you see. Such a bore.'

The formal, grown-up phrases sound absurd, artificial, but they are natural to her.

The elderly woman flinches and pats her pearls for reassurance. The child waits, holding the door, her eyes steady.

I never talked to 'other children', had no notion of how they spoke. All my words, the rich vocabulary I picked up like a matrix, duplicated; the adjectives misapplied, I drew from listening to adults. 'Inordinate', I said, and 'grotesque' and 'hilarious'. (Later, thanks to Boccaccio, I was familiar with catamites, sodomites, simony and carnal appetites.)

I once referred to Epaminondas, which made a great impression. No one could have known that I was talking not about the Theban statesman (of whom I had never heard) but about a small Negro boy in an extended morality tale often quoted by my mother, which ended with the hortatory refrain, 'Epaminondas, you ain't got the sense you was born with!' She, I suspect, had never heard of the other Epaminondas either. Or perhaps she had. She might have known a historian at some point. She knew Kulenkampff.

People reacted in different ways to this precocious prattling: sometimes it amused them, sometimes it made them uneasy. They looked narrowly at me, suspicious.

The old lady pats her pearls again, steps into the Powder Room, crosses the mushroom carpet, reaches into the closet and pulls the chain.

'Thank you,' the child says, and adds, 'I'm four.' The old lady does not respond, which is a pity because it is conversation rather than assistance that Maggie is in need of. She could have stood on the seat and pulled the chain herself, she is perfectly capable of it, but she rather wanted to talk to someone. Even more, she hoped someone might talk to her. The old lady has proved a disappointment.

Maybe if she were to tear off some more toilet paper and throw it down the bowl she could stop someone else . . . Instead she washes her hands, very thoroughly.

On this early summer evening with no breeze and birds still noisy in Russell Square, she feels the silence as a weight, a great weight forcing the breath out of her, driving her out of the pink and cream room, in search of human contact.

Behind her as she washes her hands the cistern refills, slowly, with a noise like a small waterfall. She washes her hands again. Dries them carefully. Looks in the mirror as she has seen her mother do.

Poker-straight hair is tortured into fat sausage curls all over her head; the firm, chubby body buttoned into a little red and white polka-dot dress deliberately cut a couple of inches too short, to show off the matching polka-dot knickers beneath it.

'Just like Shirley Temple,' waitresses said admiringly as they brought the tea and scones.

A lifetime later, en route to California, I found myself on the same jet as Shirley Temple – a matronly political figure by that time. She still had curly hair though, and round eyes, round cheeks. She wore a neatly buttoned suit, court shoes with cuban heels. I was going through a shaggy and ethnic phase.

I did not say: my mother wanted me to look like you; she got dressmakers to copy your little frocks, with matching knickers showing; corkscrewed my hair into your curls, broadened my dance lessons to include tap, which I never liked.

You don't tell people that sort of thing. And in any case, neatly dressed and coiffed, delicately rouged and still childishly pretty, she might well have been stunned to think that at any stage of life I could have been modelled on her, I with the sallow skin that had never recovered from that draining sun; straight, freaky hair, beads. I wondered what sort of knickers she was wearing.

In the door of the Powder Room, Maggie stands looking left and right, like someone waiting to cross a busy road.

One of the chambermaids, rounding the corner, almost trips over her. The child should be in bed. 'Come along dear, I'll see you to your room.'

She takes the small, square hand and marches along, chattering mechanically.

'Mummy out, is she? Never mind, time you were in bed, here we are . . .'

She opens the door of the suite, follows the child into the bedroom, grimly registering the spilled face-powder on the cluttered dressing table, the silk stockings and summer frock flung over a chairback, the pale coffee

41

satin and lace camiknickers in a small, shimmering heap on the carpet, the rumpled bed.

She straightens the sheets, voice purling on: 'There we are, sweet dreams, sleep tight, hope the fleas don't bite –' She glances at the child who does not smile back.

'Are there fleas here?'

The chambermaid frowns, affronted. 'Of course not! It's just a joke.'

'There are fleas, sometimes,' the child says, 'and snakes.'

The chambermaid looks at her with a mixture of suspicion and anxiety: where could they have come from? She closes the door and hurries away down the corridor.

In the bedroom, in the humming silence that encloses her like a big glass bell, Maggie begins to get undressed.

Her arms move slowly, she swims across the sub-aqueous dimness of the room. The un-noise roars softly in her ear.

'Porridge and a nice boiled egg as usual?'

'Yes, please.' She watches the waiter padding slowly away towards the kitchens. Breakfast is a good time. All around her little noises build up into a pattern of people: the discreet clatter and scrape of knives and forks on plates; the faint gurgling of tea being poured from silver pots; the crunch of toast nibbled by the old lady in pearls at the table for one against the wall; the murmur of subdued voices; the soft thud of the big, leather-covered doors leading to the kitchens.

The air too is special: the smell of hot rolls, coffee, scalded milk, bacon. Warm, heavy air that has been breathed by many people. It has a comforting staleness, nothing of the chilly morning outdoors about it.

Waiters shoulder their way through the leather doors, balancing plates and dishes on arm and wrist, exchanging terse comments as they pass each other, then thud! the doors swing closed behind them, shutting out the brief clatter and noise from the kitchen. She takes a sugar lump and slips it into her mouth. Her lips close over it, the saliva breaking down the sharp cube till it dissolves like an Indian sweetmeat, but there is no fragrance of spice or honey, just a sugary sludge without flavour.

Moti is silent, as usual at breakfast. Her face is very white this morning, with marks like faint bruises below the grey-green eyes. She glances at the newspaper without interest, long white fingers tapping impatiently, the nails dark red against the white cloth, waiting for the tea to arrive.

Maggie stares at the newspaper headline. It takes her a while, being upside down, then she gets it. Poland. Something about Poland.

'What's Poland?'

'A place.'

She wonders where it is but the waiter arrives with the tea and her porridge and she loses interest.

Instead she pours cold milk carefully into the deep plate, watching it rise like a flood round the mounds of solidly congealed porridge. Then, with a wet spoon she creates valleys, islands, lakes, a Poland within a porridge plate –

'Do stop playing with your food.' Moti is looking at her in amiable exasperation. 'And sit up.'

Her mother has a long, straight back and fine shoulders which she holds beautifully. 'Good posture improves the bustline,' she says. 'You'll grow up slouching about like a waitress which will do your bustline no good at all.'

She picks up the paper, glancing impatiently at the headlines, turning the pages quickly.

Maggie surreptitiously rolls her porridge into a smooth pebble in her mouth and swallows it unchewed, as she has seen Moti do with oysters. She looks at the waitresses, trying to see their bustline behind the aprons. This morning they forgot to bring a cushion for her, and she rests her chin on the breakfast table.

She becomes aware of a disturbance, discreet for the moment, at a table a few yards away. The young man is a fairly new arrival; she noticed him the week before. Tall, slim, with blond hair and a back as straight as Moti's. He receives fat letters in funny-looking envelopes with foreign stamps on them, and he reads them very carefully over breakfast, looking unhappy.

This morning, even before he has opened his letters he is looking unhappy. He examines his boiled egg with the intensity of a scientist. He turns the plate slowly, then pushes it sharply away from him and summons the waiter. Maggie, porridge forgotten, leans forward to listen.

'I ask,' the young man is saying in a sharp, authoritative voice with a foreign intonation, 'for a *fresh* egg.'

The waiter nods, his large feet planted heavily on the carpet. 'That's right, sir. Fresh egg. Nothing wrong with that egg.'

The young man's face is crimson. 'I ask for a fresh egg and you bring me an egg from *Lithuania*.' He points accusingly at something stamped on the egg. 'See! *Not* fresh. *Not* English. Maybe from a *Jewish* chicken!'

The waiter, apologizing, sweeps the egg away and flees through the leather doors. The young man glances about him angrily until he catches Maggie's undisguised stare. He stops, stares back at her frostily for a moment and then, unexpectedly, sticks out his tongue.

Delighted, she glances quickly to check that Moti is absorbed in the newspaper and sticks out her tongue in return. The young man raises his cup to her, sips his tea and turns to his first letter.

*

44

I had never seen a beach. The sea was something you looked at over a ship's rail, dark, clean blue, foaming into a creamy wake. But this pale, bright expanse with white frills collapsing repeatedly onto smooth, flat sand – an enormous version of the sandpit I played in under the tamarind tree at Amaryllis – this landscape of striped deck-chairs and changing huts, of sunshades and sports cars, all under a gentle sun that sparkled on water and turned skin rosy and golden, this was quite new and different.

The hotel, Russell Square, the taxis and the park had been abandoned. This was Dorset, something called 'the seaside' which I had read about. This was a holiday.

Alexander had friends who owned a beach house in a sheltered bay. Someone kept saying that Douglas Fairbanks should be arriving soon, and someone else, a man with an American accent, talked about Technicolor a lot and told me that soon all the movies would be in colour. 'Black and white's as dead as the silents,' he said, usually after three cocktails.

Each morning we poured out of the big house which seemed to be all windows and glass doors, onto the beach. Everyone wore swimsuits and my mother's long legs and small breasts looked their best. She swam, with me clinging to her back, out to a raft, where we lay, she with eyes closed, I watching the movement of water as it rocked the raft, endlessly sucking and rejecting it, slapping gently aginst the wooden struts.

We ate ice-cream and played complicated, silly games, ran wheelbarrow races and made a good deal of noise. I was walked out to sea on the shoulders of the man who was waiting for Douglas Fairbanks; far, far out until his head bobbed below the surface and I seemed to be sitting on the sea itself.

There were older children, who taught me how to build sand-castles and how to swim, dog-paddling in

45

the shallow waves, and when the man who talked about Technicolor heard that I could dance he told Moti he could get me into pictures: cute kids with English accents and dancing ability were good currency.

'She could earn big money . . . they're looking for a new Shirley Temple . . .' He was serious, but Moti refused to take him seriously. Until she caught him auditioning me, getting me to show off my dancing skills, which did not greatly impress him, and my singing, which did.

'Hey, the kid can carry a line!' He sounded approving.

She was sharp with him: she did not wish to pursue the question of Maggie's becoming a film star. Margaret-Rose might become a ballet-dancer one day. She certainly hoped so. We were looking for a good dancing teacher. But Hollywood – no. In Hollywood she knew what happened to children: they became highly paid slaves, ruining their lives with false values, unnatural activities and nervous disorders. No. The subject was closed.

In Dorset the sun continued to shine, the sea to splash gently on the sand. Sometimes, in a conjunction of sounds and sensations, it comes back so vividly that I am there again. Heraclitus is denied: I step into the same shallow waves, feel them tickle my bare legs. The salt dries on my skin, scaly, stiffening the hairs. Sand grits beneath my teeth.

In my ears, all jumbled up together, I hear shouts and good-humoured argument; voices calling the score in a game of beach badminton, a wobbly tune played on a wind-up gramophone, and my mother laughing.

She laughs, head flung back, eyes closed, mouth open, lying carelessly on the warm sand, and I run back and forth along the line of surf, laughing too, without reason.

*   *   *

46

It is meals rather than clock chimes which mark the passing of the hours in a hotel. Not just the food itself, but the sounds and smells that accompany its preparation. By the moist, warm, vanilla-laden fragrance rising from the kitchens Maggie can tell it is tea-time.

She watches her mother dressing: an eau-de-nil frock of silk crepe today, its surface finely wrinkled like the cheek of an old lady.

I watch the child watching the woman.

The eau-de-nil dress has a flurry of frills round the low neckline; they curl and move like waves breaking on the dunes of her small breasts. She applies make-up; picks up a cut-glass bottle and presses the bulb of a silken cord to release sprays of 'Ma Griffe'.

'I like your perfume.'

'Don't say perfume,' she says mechanically. 'It's scent. I've told you before.' They go down to tea.

People are filtering slowly in to take their places at their usual tables in the lounge. Guests staying only a few days are more tentative, waiting to be shown where to sit.

As the waiter takes their order and moves off, Maggie sees the young man of the Lithuanian egg episode approaching. He bows, clicking his heels slightly, formal, correct.

'May I join you?'

Moti glances up at him, tilting back her head, looking down her long nose, cool. She smiles.

But alas, she is about to leave; she has an engagement. She has come into the lounge only to order tea for her daughter. He nods.

'However, I would be honoured to join the young lady for tea.'

Moti looks surprised. He clicks his heels again, presents himself formally. Moti considers the matter: the young man is attractive; there will be days when she is not otherwise engaged. She decides he is acceptable and

47

offers her own name. 'And my daughter, Margaret-Rose.'

She leaves, the waiter arrives with the first of the plates and together they watch the buttered toast, the pastries, the china being assembled, giving it their full attention.

'Margaret-Rose,' he says, offering her a plate of minute sandwiches, 'that is a pretty name for a pretty little girl. In my country we sing a song about Rose Marie. I shall call you Rose Marie.'

Maggie, who has never been called pretty by anyone as far as she can remember, stares at the tall, blond, blue-eyed man without smiling. She sees that he has small scars on his face, white against the tanned skin.

'How old are you, Rose Marie?'

'Five,' she says. 'Can you sing that song, the one about Rose Marie?'

'Oh yes.'

Usually at tea-time a trio occupied the dais with the potted palms but they were late today, still tuning up their instruments. He leaned forward and very softly, in a light, clear tenor, began to sing the tango that was everywhere that summer of 1939:

> *'Oh, Rose Marie, I love you;*
> *I'm always dreaming of you . . .'*

On days when her mother is busy Maggie no longer has solitary tea in the lounge because Otto joins her. On other days, if he has spent the afternoon in the British Museum Reading Room, where he puts in a good deal of time, they pass a sociable hour together after dinner, discussing England, and his own country, which he misses, but not so much, it seems, that he is in a hurry to return to it.

'One day I will have to return, to fly my aeroplane.

Unless I stay here; perhaps I stay here, at the British Museum.' He laughs.

When they have finished their chat and it is time for him to change for dinner, or for Maggie to go to bed, always she requests, 'Will you sing my song?'

And she stands by his knee while his soft voice, very low, goes through the song:

'*Oh, Rose Marie, I love you . . .*'

So weeks of summer pass. And one afternoon, coming in, elated, from a visit to the cinema (Dorothy Lamour and Preston Foster in *Moonlight and Roses*, not an offering Moti has particularly enjoyed) Maggie sees Otto already in the lounge, reading a letter. She leaves her mother at the foot of the shallow, curving staircase and runs across the room to greet him. The thick carpet deadens the sound of her footsteps, and he is still deep in his letter and unaware of her presence until she cries, 'Sing me the song!'

Otto jerks his head up, startled. For a moment he stares at the child without recognition. Then he slowly begins to fold the letter. He replaces it in the envelope with the German stamps. He looks grim.

'Sing me the song!'

He looks at her blankly. 'What?'

She seizes his hand, tugs it impatiently, confidently. '*You* know! Oh, Rose Marie, I love you! Sing it!'

He looks sour, exhausted, but still not sensing the change in him the child bangs her fist on his knee, chanting, 'Come *on*, sing the *song*, sing Rose Marie, I love you!'

'No.' His voice is sharp, irritable. 'I have to go now. Besides, I don't love you. You are a silly little girl, do not bother me.'

For a moment the child thinks it is a game and her smile widens. Then, looking at his eyes, she sees he

49

means it, and her hand drops from his knee. The smile droops, dies, leaving her mouth hanging open in dismay. She feels a stony coldness creeping up her body as though the ground were chilling her, until finally she begins to shiver uncontrollably.

She swallows quickly, several times, then turns and walks across the lounge, past the table with the trays, past bread and butter and pastries and toast cut in triangles.

On the stairs she meets her mother coming down.

'I thought I would join you,' Moti says gaily. 'We can have tea with your nice young man.'

She looks so cheerful, so fresh and at one with the world that Maggie feels unable to shatter the rare radiance, to pull the smiling mouth into a disappointed downward curve.

So she just shrugs her shoulders as she has seen Moti do so often, and shakes her head.

'I don't want any tea today, thank you.'

In the bedroom she closes the door carefully. She hears the humming silence enter her head, feels the glass bell enclose her. The silence roars softly through the room.

Moti's parents did not live together. This scarcely seemed unusual to me: *my* parents spent much of their time apart. But Moti would not see her father: she held him responsible for her marriage. His mistrust, his denunciation of the lascivious brown eyes had started it all. He had forbidden the marriage, which merely made her more determined. And then, forbidding the wedding, he had been defied. She went ahead and married the undesirable young man anyway. Something wrong here: to ignore his interdiction she would have to be over the age of consent. So I cannot have been born when she was twenty. Already the ground is shifting; her adjustments of history, her rearranging of factual furniture alters the perspective.

But I can vouch for some of it. For example: we were leaving the hotel in Russell Square to visit Moti's mother. Alexander had been busy, it seemed. There had been fewer trips. Life had grown dull.

Moti's mother has made Maggie a costume from cut-up gold damask curtains, a Spanish affair with a long, full skirt and a sort of lace mantilla.

She lives in a small cottage in an undistinguished village – almost a town – in Essex. She is a medium-sized woman, shorter than her daughter, and rounder, with none of that equine elegance. She and the child become friends at once and Maggie trails round the cottage as she tidies it, watching her. It is the first time she has seen anyone other than servants do housework of any sort.

Her grandmother folds up clothes, puts them away, dusts surfaces; this is part of her daily activity. It takes up a great deal of time and Maggie finds it extraordinary. She follows her, repeating her actions.

Moti was away in London. Perhaps Alexander had stopped being busy, had reappeared with seats for the opera? We came to Essex by train, which I enjoyed more than she did, exploring corridors, lavatories, touching the velvety pile of the upholstery. At the station we waited for the one taxi. Moti fretted, accustomed to a better class of transport.

Today she would face the train again, unless Alexander drove her in the Bentley. She was due home at six and I was already dressed in my gold costume at five. We had concocted a special supper to surprise her, Grannie and I: the *pièce de résistance* a trick dessert – half a tinned peach surrounded by very thick cream, thinly sliced tinned pear, arranged on a plate to look like fried egg and bacon.

'I cooked it specially for you,' I planned to say, and watch her face as she tasted it.

Everything is ready by six, table laid, tinned peaches tricked out with cream, smoked salmon under a damp cloth, three different salads.

At eight they decide to eat some of the feast, picking at the edges of plates so that they do not spoil the appearance. Around nine Grannie falls asleep in her wooden armchair. Maggie must have done the same for she sits up suddenly, her feet numb, mantilla slipped sideways, as the front door slams. It is eleven o'clock.

Moti appears in the doorway of the tiny front room. She looks odd, her cheeks and eyes very bright.

Before she can speak, Grannie begins to shout: no consideration . . . totally selfish . . . she has had time to prepare the words and there are a good many of them. The brightness fades from Moti's face, it begins to stiffen into the hard, scornful lines of Beethoven nights at Amaryllis.

'Oh, let's have the special supper then, for God's sake,' she says. She glances over the table, at the curled sandwiches, the limp salads. The juice from the tinned peaches has done funny things to the cream and the trick dessert no longer looks the part. Moti stares at it, baffled.

'What on earth is that?'

'Fried egg peach,' Maggie explains. 'That's cream, and slices of pear painted to look like bacon – it's all right, we used cochineal –'

'What I would really love,' she says, 'is a cup of tea,' and begins to cry, crumbling slowly into tears as though

52

too tired to hold them off. Maggie finds her a handkerchief, her mother makes the tea. By midnight it is a feast after all, but she does not eat the peach.

'We're going to Brighton,' Moti said. Not on a visit, but to stay for a while. Essex had not proved congenial. And no one mentioned Alexander any more.

What went wrong? Was there a cool Scottish fiancée somewhere, a wife even? Moti no more than that sad sexual cliché, the ship-board romance? Or perhaps she herself destroyed the picture he had of her, revealing the dark shadow, the edgy note we lived with at home.

What if . . .? I used to wonder. What if Alexander had come zooming down to Essex in the Bentley and –

As always there was no post-mortem, no questions and certainly no answers. As was her way, she shrugged things off with a joke. 'Bloody bagpipes,' she said à propos nothing in particular, one day. 'Just because one comes from Dundee doesn't mean one has to like *bagpipes*. I ask you.'

There had been a second trip to London, but after that she stayed at the cottage, spending mornings in bed, getting up late and walking into the village 'for some fresh air'.

In the King's Head she struck up the easy friendships of the cocktail bars at home. I kept forgetting that of course *this* was home too.

Confusing, difficult to work out where we really belonged to, now. Waiting for her outside the Lounge entrance I heard the same mysterious, blurred conversation, the sudden explosions of laughter, the silences of bottled conviviality.

She brought me orange drinks and crisps in a bag with a blue paper screw of salt, and later we walked

53

back to the cottage. She strode ahead with that loping gait, handbag wedged in armpit.

I watched her haunches move, the quiver of her bare calves and the roughened heels slipping about on the high sling-back sandals.

I had never noticed her feet looking unkempt before – surely they never were; this was something new. She always painted her toenails scarlet to match her fingers, she showed off her high arches. But now the bright red varnish was chipped and flaking, the skin looked dry.

'Brighton will do us good,' she said, eyes bright from King's Head companionship. 'You'll like it, you like the seaside.'

So Brighton, like Dorset, was seaside. But how different! No sand. No laughing companions. No lazy days spent in swimsuits, rolling like puppies in the hot sand. Brighton was London with sea breezes.

Moti rented a flat at Black Rock and I found myself attending dancing classes at Roedean school, up on the cliffs. This was not usual, but Moti knew someone who knew someone else who made it possible.

Before long she had bought school uniform for me, enjoying a new area of fantasy: 'Margaret-Rose is at Roedean – she's too young of course, but she's precocious, well she read *Gulliver's Travels* when she was three . . .'

A flat was less agreeable than a hotel: no one brought breakfast to the table, no one slipped in, unseen, to tidy the room and change the sheets.

Moti did the cooking, throwing food together casually, with careless flair. We ate on the corners of the cluttered table or on the sofa, plates balanced on knees.

Moti did the cooking . . . but what did she cook? When did she do it? I have no memory of her at gas stove or sink. I can see only our walks along the front,

54

or to the end of the pier, me in my polka-dot Shirley Temple frock with matching panties, her in something she called a playsuit, a sort of one-piece top and flared shorts made of floppy silk.

Her hair frizzed in the damp sea air and her pale legs were goose pimpled. She did not look her best. But before long, a new man had joined us, her back had straightened and her smile was flashing like a beacon.

In the morning, without lipstick, mascara, eye-shadow, rouge, foundation, powder; hair in a Suzanne Lengleng bandeau, her face is pale and undefined. Without the paint and the pencils she is more touchable, gentler, frail, like an undernourished horse, and she laughs differently.

Her eyes, too, are different: they look amused, sad, tired. Later, after a jaunt with the new man they are brighter, but with a glassy sheen that replaces expression. They are brilliant but blank.

On wet days they go to the Aquarium. It is dim, cool, echoing. It has a smell of its own: a mixture of damp underground caves and hospital disinfectant.

They walk past the fish tanks in the greenish, wavering light, hearing the murmuring sound of water. Occasionally the water is disturbed by a frilly stream of escaping bubbles as some creature dives to the shallow bottom. The stone floor is chilly to the visitors' feet.

There are crocodiles motionless, seeming asleep until an eye flickers, watchful. Maggie worries about her mother's handbag: can a crocodile recognize a fellow croc's skin, cut up and fashioned? Might it inspire a sudden burst of energy, a smashing of glass, a gobbling of mother and daughter . . .? She positions herself discreetly in front of the bag.

In one glass case a turtle sits on a flat stone. He seems

55

always to be in the same place and Maggie thinks he looks lost, abandoned.

The man who runs the Aquarium is a friend of Moti's; she sees him occasionally in the Lounge Bar, and she chats to him when she comes in with Maggie. He keeps an eye on the child when she is left alone to wander there while Moti goes off on one of her little jaunts. He is kind – she has a gift for picking out kind strangers and yoking them to the problem on hand: 'Keep an eye on the child, would you? I worry dreadfully about her . . .'

The turtle looks lonely. His eyes are as dull as his grey, wrinkled skin. Maggie stares in at him but his gaze is unfocused. She raps gently on the glass to attract his attention, but the glass is too thick.

For a moment she thinks of the dancing bear, the shaggy, dusty fur and the rust-coloured eyes that looked back, dulled . . .

'You all right, kiddo?' The man who runs the Aquarium puts a large, moist hand on her shoulder. She can feel the heat of his hand through the thin cotton.

'Yes, thank you. Perfectly all right.'

He wanders on. She taps the glass case again, but inside, sealed behind his glass wall, the turtle cannot hear her.

Moti had never mentioned a brother. Now we were on our way to visit him, perhaps to stay for a while. For how long?

'That depends.'

Pointless to continue questioning. 'That depends' was like 'perhaps' or 'we shall see': it meant an end to the discussion.

The countryside flew past; the train whistle shrilled. It was warm and cosy as we rocked and swayed up the spine of England. I watched her face in the glass of the window: soot and dust covered her reflection so that she appeared grubby, begrimed, her face a scarecrow image beating at the pane to be allowed in out of the wind and the rain. Repelled, shocked, I flung myself away from the window, round to the woman sitting opposite, for reassurance. Her mouth drooped. She stared at the window, not seeing the countryside. It was rare to catch her like this, alone with her thoughts in daylight, cut off from cocktail bar vivacity, friends, music, sudden laughter.

Her hair was only slightly disarrayed, lipstick only a little smudged, but with a twinge of horror I saw that the window reflection was not completely false. She moved, caught my eye and smiled, straightening her shoulders. She raised her eyebrows, half-squinting down her long nose ironically, exiling the reflection to where it belonged, out there in the cold and the rain.

'Tea in the restaurant car, shall we? Toast and butter? A little treat?'

Scotland was different. The wind was sharper and the porridge was better, though they put salt not sugar on it, and everyone talked like Alexander, lilting and singing their words, making them special.

This was the homeground of Moti's father, the eminent architect, and we did not mention Grannie in her cottage down in Essex. Nor did we mention Moti's father, whom I never met. For her he had long ago become the enemy.

In the draughty hall hung old family photographs, the women plump and composed, the men black-clad and narrow. The houses in those photographs were palatial and the faces of the men stern but at the same time complacent. In later photographs the houses were more modest. I studied figures in deck-chairs, or

57

grouped outside front doors, trying to link up faces: Grannie and the eminent architect must have been a couple once, but the features were too indistinct and I knew that it would not do to ask.

I noticed that Moti wore one of her plainer outfits and somewhere along the line had removed her scarlet nail polish. I decided to be especially polite and helpful. Later that day I heard my uncle's wife comment that the bairn seemed peculiar, maybe a little soft in the head.

My uncle's reply was not unsympathetic. 'It's not her fault. Look at the background. I fear the worst.'

What background? What did he fear? And for whom? More mysteries.

That was the last day of August, and there were no more murmured conversations, covert glances at the visitors. Instead, a keen studying of the newspaper and listening to the wireless and everyone talking about Germany and Poland.

'Where's Lithuania?' I asked, but no one was listening.

The row blew up that night.

Maggie is already in bed. There are voices raised below, over-riding each other, mixed up so that she cannot hear properly what is being said.

'You can leave the child –'

' – ridiculous –'

' – better for her –'

' – my own affair –'

' – a proper home –'

' – mausoleum –'

' – bad example –'

' – bloody hell! –'

A door bangs. The light snaps on in the guest bedroom.

'We're leaving,' Moti says. 'Get dressed.'

She walks to the station with the child. Her brother

does not offer to drive them, and she does not ask him to.

'I carried you all the way to the station,' Moti told me, years later, 'in a snowstorm. The bastard wouldn't drive us. Cold, they're cold as granite, all of them.'

A *snowstorm*? Could this be? Surely it was still summer? True, this was Scotland, but –

'All the way to the station. And my arthritis was giving me hell, but you couldn't walk in that weather, just a mite, so I carried you . . .'

I began to see us as she described it: stumbling down that granite street, her, thin and indomitable, the small child clutched to her bosom as light darkens and the snow flurries drive against her face, sharp as blades.

I have no other memory but that description – unreliable, of course, but vivid. One thing I do recall: nobody said goodbye.

We lived much in hotels, my mother and I. Some grand, others less so. As money ran low we moved down the scale, from Park Lane to Russell Square, to Bayswater. There were 'Guest Houses', genteel, respectable; there were 'Rooms'. There was a boarding house for poor whites run by Armenians – loud, flamboyant, tactile people who shouted at each other and the guests, and who gave me a banana before throwing us out. But that was later.

For the moment it was a faceless London hotel with a double bed and a big geyser in the bathroom with copper pipes that hissed, and steaming water spluttering and gushing from a spout over the green-stained bath.

Moti was unaccustomed to such primitive artifacts. She managed without a bath for a day or two, but then a personable man in the hotel bar suggested dinner. She turned on the geyser tap and hurried out of the bathroom, winding her hair into curlers, laying out clothes and undressing. Then she tested the water.

'Blast. It's cold. The pilot must be out.'

I watched, standing by the door as she struck a match, stooped to light the pilot and swing it into position over the gas jets – which had been turned on some time before. The geyser exploded with a roar and the blast ripped across the room exactly level with my eyes. As it hit me, the ceiling came down, raining chunks of plaster into the bath. The plaster and I crashed to the floor together.

The doctor was sure my sight would not be permanently impaired; the damage to the cornea was superficial. Meanwhile I was led about, eyes bandaged like a Bombay beggar. I heard Moti say to some invisible acquaintance, 'The Child's always having these extraordinary accidents – she ran bang into a mirror once.'

I have just made up those words. I have no recollection of her saying this. In fact, what is more probable is that she led me about with my bandaged eyes, cosseting me publicly, winning sympathy from everyone.

'Poor little mite' – 'mite' was one of her words – 'isn't it bloody? And she's being so good about it.'

I was always 'good about it', whatever it was. Why? I knew tantrums, tears, would get me nowhere, was that it? Or was it because I dimly felt she had enough to worry about already? Or perhaps to win golden opinions. I was generally considered a very good little girl. No trouble to anyone.

Moti, standing right next to the geyser, bending down to peer in at the unlit gas jets, was unhurt, just covered in thick white dust. She could have been killed, I reflected often, later. With regret, disappointment, dull bitterness I used to think: she could have been killed.

The doctor was right, no permanent damage, though I had to wear funny little metal spectacles with dark

60

lenses for a while. It took longer to convince me that geysers were not always dangerous: when Moti struck a match in the bathroom, I dived under the bed.

But my accident did not arouse much excitement, how could it? I had chosen a bad time: war, whatever that meant, had been declared.

Moti began to pack. 'We're going home.'

Home? But *this* had been home. Hadn't she said, 'We're going home on a visit'? But now, it seemed, home was where we had started from.

*   *   *

Three of us at Lucknow station. The car waiting. They stood on either side of me, not touching.

His shirt had dark half-moons of sweat beneath the armpits. Moti in pale linen and a hat looked cool, as though standing in her own private breeze.

'How was the crossing?'

'Oh, fairly average.'

'No trouble with –'

'No, no.'

He picked me up, looked at me, still in my metal spectacles. She had long since given up attempting to make my hair curl and it lay unbecomingly flat and straight round my face.

He swallowed a couple of times, staring at me.

'You've grown a bit.'

'Not much, I'm afraid.'

'Oh yes, definitely. Grown. And too thin.'

A murmur from Moti, 'Criticizing already? That'll help the Child's confidence.'

'I wasn't criticizing the Child.' He put me down.

The war had brought us home. But home was very strange. I had forgotten how dusty and dry the compound was, the way the tamarind pods hung down from the dusty branches like strips of dried meat. I had

61

forgotten the clean, fresh bed with newly washed and ironed sheets every night.

There was a song Moti used to sing, one verse of which went:

> *What care I for my goose-feather bed,*
> *With the sheet turned down so bravely-O?*
> *For tonight I shall sleep in a cold open field,*
> *Along with the Wraggle-Taggle Gypsies-O!*

Well, *I* cared.

It all quickly became normal: the ayah to lay out clothes twice a day; meals at a long polished table with different glasses for different drinks. Matching plates. The quiet evenings filled with humming silence, and later, the voices in the night.

They would come home from the club and it would begin: the shouting, the crying.

Moti, it seemed, was often in pain of various sorts: her headaches, her arthritis. She was prescribed belladonna.

The belladonna bottle is small and dark blue, the inky blue of her silk dress with the halter neck. It has a rubber bulb top and a glass dropper. The rubber is brownish red like dried blood. She is told she must take care to measure out the drops accurately and dilute the dose with water.

In the morning she squeezes the bulb gently, the glass tube sucks up the belladonna and the drops, one . . . two . . . swirl in the glass of water. At night she threatens to take it all – 'Swallow the lot, why not? What's the point?' and she runs shrieking from the house. He runs after her, out across the compound, down to the deserted road. He pursues her, they fight over the blue glass bottle and he wrests it from her, flings it away, the glass smashing against a wall with a small tinkling noise.

Not that night, but sometimes, she strikes him: twice across the face, forehand, backhand. The sound is like cracks of a whip. He never hits back, nor does he cry or fall to his knees as others do, later. He is silent, his face expressionless.

These incidents always take place at night. The child hears the voices, catches glimpses, retreats. Then, like a roaring in her ears, the silence blanks out the voices. The glass bell descends. She slides slowly into a tunnel . . . darkness . . . numbness. She watches herself, unreachable. Her head turns, slowly. An arm, a leg, the movements are endlessly prolonged, slowed down. Inconveniently, disconcertingly, the nightmare recurs in daylight hours, like the malaria that surfaces regularly in her body, year after year.

In daylight the mood is different: he goes off to the mill, Moti to the club or to swim. She remains detached from her surroundings, bored in the company of Indians – ordinary Indians, that is. An old acquaintance, a maharaja encountered at the races, is more congenial. Public school, charming, ready with banter . . . Her eyes flicker gold and green, she laughs, she makes him laugh. They have much in common: he too is bored in the company of ordinary Indians.

The war, it seemed, was going on elsewhere. Here, the riots continued, and Moti fulminated against 'that bloody man Gandhi'. She worried most about the Russians. 'It's not the Germans I'm bothered about, we can deal with them. But the Russians could be down through Afghanistan and here in no time.'

'The Russians are on our side, Moti,' someone pointed out to her once.

'So they say,' she said darkly. Perched on a high bar-stool she displayed a lot of her legs in the short skirts that had replaced the bias-cut droopy frocks that suited her so well.

Meanwhile, the riots. And the hot weather. Everyone went to the hills when the hot weather came. It was usual. Why then did it feel so bad, this time, when we prepared to go?

Car, station, train. They stood either side of me, looming, speaking of everyday things. The house. The servants. The child.

What was it they said about the child? Should I have listened more carefully?

Later Maggie is informed crucial decisions have been made. Decisions in which she is supposed to have played a part. But why can she remember none of it? All she knows is that one day, when they seem to have been away long enough, she asks when they are going home, and Moti says calmly, 'Daddy and I have decided to live apart.'

The child waits to be told what this means. Moti hugs her cheerfully. 'Don't worry. You're staying with me.'

'What about Daddy?'

'He'll be at Amaryllis.'

'Shan't I see him?'

'You chose to stay with me.'

I *chose*? When did I choose? I think back; try to recall this all-important moment. I find hotels and quarrels; swimming pools and hot buttered toast; riots and train journeys. I find magic and moving shadows. In a house with a tree-shaded garden I find a wedding where a bride in silk, with silver tears painted on her cheeks, waits for an unknown husband. Sunflowers. Sweetmeats crumbling on the tongue. I can find nothing that says 'I choose'.

*

At the beginning it was not so different. Everyone, after all, went to the hills in the hot season. As always, Moti made new friends and Maggie – 'she'd much rather have her nose in a book' – was left behind while the rickshaw took Moti spinning down the hillside on one of her jaunts.

But gradually changes took place. Little by little Moti cut us off from polite society. Not right away; we moved from one hill station to another, one guest house to another, so it took time. But there was never a return visit to the Residents' Club; never a second invitation to tea/supper/tiffin.

There was a terrible inevitability about these occasions. Moti, newly arrived, would be charming, seem vulnerable, perhaps pathetic. A slight mystery was not unwelcome in a social pond where there were few ripples. She must be taken up. And the child, of course. Odd little thing. Silent. Too old for her age. But still . . .

Then came the invitation. And the acceptance. Gracious: 'How kind. We'd love to.'

Moti would ransack the suitcase for some outfit befitting the time of day. She would probably wash, certainly make up carefully. Have a little drink to fortify herself. Possibly a second. Eyes a little glassy now, walk more jaunty, handbag tucked firmly beneath her arm, she would arrive and welcome the kindly patronage of hostess and friends for a while. If it was tea-time, presently she would go off to powder her nose.

The child watches her go with dread: nose-powdering, in her experience, leads to a change of mood.

Back comes Moti, eyes a little glassier, expression beginning to settle into the grim, dissatisfied lines the child has learned to look out for. There is usually trouble within twenty minutes of the nose-powdering. It takes different forms: on one occasion a casual obscenity, another time an unacceptable frankness. Here it comes, now:

65

'Oops. Bloody hell. Spilt the tea. Still, it won't show on that God-awful rug, will it?'

Awkwardness spreads like the spilt tea and the party breaks up early. They wait for a rickshaw or walk, Moti loping ahead, fast, tigerish, the child raging silently: if they had stayed longer they might have talked more. About school, for instance. There must be a school here.

And school, more than anything in the world, is what I longed for. My favourite reading (*pace* Moti) was not Swift but Angela Brazil. Wonderful stories of safe adventures that ended in laughter and congratulations. Oh, well done, Maggie! Retrieved the school cup from burglars *and* got top marks in the exam! Paradise.

But clearly the time for school is not yet. Back in the bedroom Moti throws down the handbag with its small, flattish bulge. The bag is lighter now. And Moti is roaring. Those bitches with their neatly permed hair, their averted eyes, who the hell did they think they were? She could play the piano, speak two foreign languages, her father was an eminent architect. She was damned if she would fit into their dreary suburban pigeonhole.

And the child weeps, craving a suburban pigeonhole. There will be no invitation to meet little Sally or Lizzie as promised; no children's party at the club. Once again they are outside the walls.

My children love *Alice in Wonderland*. This is because they have led an ordered existence and consequently enjoy the swooping uncertainties, the surrealism of *Alice*. I hated it. How should I not? It was my story, a frighteningly accurate reflection of my everyday anxieties. This was no fantasy of dreamland. For me, too, things changed constantly, bewilderingly. People became hostile, flight necessary. I seemed, like Alice, to change my shape and identity with unsettling results.

How big are you? I'm not quite sure, Alice replied . . . How old are you? people asked me. I was never quite sure what age Moti had decided on for that week. I hesitated. I must have seemed a very peculiar little girl.

Quite soon I knew the book almost by heart; Alice's universe was one of insecurity and arbitrary change. She changes size, shape, identity, betrayed by familiar objects. Shut out of the beautiful garden at the end of the tunnel. The gold key was out of reach – or useless. She had no one near her who was trustworthy. But all that was my everyday life. I did not need some writer to make it up for me. 'No room! No room!'

Like Alice I wanted someone ordinary and reasonable to talk to. Ordinariness was what I craved. Moti was a combination of Red Queen, Duchess and Mad Hatter: like them, she seemed ruled by a logic not available to the rest of us. Like the beasts in the story she lamented some unspecified tragedy, some sad tale told by the seashore in the violet dusk. On most days she was filled with incommunicable woe and alcohol in equal parts. I suspect that she too found it useful to believe in six impossible things before breakfast.

One morning she appeared, dressed entirely in black, lipstick a gash in a face whiter even than nature had provided. A tragedy queen. I asked no questions. By this time I had learned that was not the way. We walked to the cocktail bar, a little late, so her friends were already assembled.

Grand entrance: alarm, concern, questions. She blinks back tears.

'Bad news, I'm afraid . . . my brother's Spitfire . . . shot down . . . missing, presumed killed . . .'

There had been no post. No telephone call. She had received no visitor. How could she possibly know this?

How then could it be true? But the grief, the suffering seemed so genuine. It was almost as though her suffering built up inside her until she had to find a reason to express it to stop herself going mad.

She ordered a double and got down to some serious mourning.

With the cooler weather the exodus began: the Memsahibs and the children trickled back to husbands and fathers and waiting bungalows. They packed up trunks and their servants loaded rickshaws and moved them painlessly from hillside to railway station to home.

We too were about to move on. The main reason was Moti's boredom. There *were* men in the hill station, but the choice was limited, as were the social opportunities: some were convalescing from a bad bout of jaundice or malaria, others were on leave. She generally laid claim to the healthy ones without delay. One day they would be playing bridge or attending a cocktail party at the Residents' Club, the next, there they were, down in one of the town bars, hanging on her bright, flippant words, roaring. The next steps were more faltering, but they led in the end to her bedroom at the guest house.

It is late afternoon when her mother appears on the veranda with a companion in tow. A guest who has come for tea, it is explained.

From the garden, Maggie peers at the guest: he is a serviceman, she can tell that even without the uniform. He has already made his unsteady way indoors, but she had time to notice his bright ginger hair.

The ladies who run the guest house have no way of dealing with the situation; there is no house rule to be invoked, no notice to be pointed at – 'Men may not be brought back to the rooms' – because such a thing has never happened before. No one could have thought the matter would come up. Respectable women simply did not bring men back with them – or they have not, till now.

So a tea-tray is ordered and sent to the room, and the door is closed.

This will be one of those afternoons the child spends wandering the hillsides, squatting down with locals, watching them cook, hearing their stories.

There are astonishing flowers which grow wild on the hillsides. She picks them and presses them in the pages of a book which belongs to the guest house, *Vanity Fair*. She does not read it: the print is small, the pages look dull, but it makes a perfect flower press: thick, with strong, heavy covers.

There are stones of strange shapes and colours which lie beside the track; some have been worn smooth by time and weather so that they glimmer like polished gems. These she picks up and keeps. There is always the possibility that one might turn out to be a precious stone, to be sold for a vast sum, to pay for railway tickets, school fees.

It is already growing dark by the time she returns to the guest house, and there is no sound from inside their room. She waits, listening, for a while. They must have gone back into town. She opens the bedroom door: the room is dark, half-drawn curtains throw shadows onto whitewashed walls. On the bed lie her mother and the guest. The sheets are twisted, pulled partly off the mattress. Her mother sleeps in her favourite position: on her stomach, knees drawn up in a sideways twist. She is breathing heavily. Her guest lies on his back, spreadeagled, one arm flung out across Mo's neck. His face is in shadow but Maggie can see now that his beard, like his hair, is bright ginger. At his crotch, a ginger bush catches the light, and his pink, flaccid member lolls, spent and shrunk. There have been many guests in many guest houses but Maggie realizes that this is the first time she has actually seen one in possession of the territory. She sees with irritation that he is occupying her side of the bed.

My mother, as I said, owned one record and two books. The *Decameron* she hid among her clothes at the bottom of the wardrobe. Omar Khayyám she read aloud from, quoted and lived by. The moving finger wrote frequently in our company, and having writ, moved on – but not far.

> *Come fill the Cup and in the Fire of Spring*
> *The Winter Garment of Repentance fling;*
> *The Bird of Time has but a little way*
> *To Fly – and Lo! the Bird is on the Wing.*

There was a sentimental self-identification there: The Flask of wine, the book of verse and Thou/Beside me, singing in the Wilderness . . . There was always a flask of wine – or at least a half of gin. The 'thou' – though face and name might change – was generally beneath the bough as well.

The book was bad enough; the record was inescapable. I knew the day had begun when I heard the gramophone handle being wound up, and I fell asleep to its wheezing sound, the words of 'Gloomy Sunday' reaching me through bunched-up bedclothes.

It was a terrible song: it certainly inspired terror and dread in at least one listener. It was a hymn to death and dying and she put it on the wind-up gramophone every day for a year and played it over and over and over again. I must have heard it two thousand times. And if you tell me that no 78 can survive two thousand playings, I know only that it did, though there was more hiss than Holiday by the end, and for all I know she may have gone out and bought a replacement at some stage.

However she managed it, there it was: a dirge that stopped me sleeping, that woke me up. I loathed it.

Sunday is gloomy, my hours are slumberless;
Dearest, the shadows I live with are numberless.
Little white flowers will never awaken you.
Not where the black coach of sorrow has taken you.
Angels have no thought of ever returning you;
Would they be angry if I thought of joining you?
Gloomy Sunday . . .

I hated the slow, drag-footed pace, the note of despair, the images the words conjured up.

I was haunted by funeral processions, black-plumed horses, waxy lilies that drowned you in their sweetness, women in subfusc garments staring out of high windows, open graves and grinning skulls.

Doom laden, it washed over Moti like a scathing surf: she knew the pull of that tide; her overdose threats, the swimming pool farewells, were a flirtation with danger and self-destruction.

And perhaps she knew, instinctively, that this was a last plateau, the point at which her tenuous connection with respectability was to be severed.

So she listened, and I listened too. The skulls hovered over my bed and reminded me of the man on the boat, the yellow teeth, and I sweated in terror.

Wind up the handle, set the needle, pour the gin and listen. 'Gloomy Sunday', that whining cadence, and gin clear as water.

The bottles themselves smelled of herbs and spices when I sniffed them, but neat gin on the breath was different: a sweetish, sickly smell, a smell of putrefaction and staleness that I grew to know so well that my

71

stomach heaved in instant recognition as I opened the front door.

The bottles were everywhere, but always out of sight: stuffed in suitcases, in cupboards and drawers, beneath beds, tucked under pillows. In breadbin and linen basket, on top of wardrobes, inside boots and shopping bags. Mostly they were empty. The full one was generally wrapped in brown paper, or swaddled in an old cardigan. Halves were useful: they fitted inside a handbag. Portable courage.

'Down the hatch . . .'

And Billie sang on. Listening to that sad song hour after hour, day after day, month after month, I not only knew it by heart, I picked up the phrasing and timing, the exact delivery of a jazz singer whose name meant nothing to me then. I heard the way she took a melody and gently teased and twisted it, stretching a high note, then letting go, dropping into a sound that was little more than a breath, a caress, tugging against the formal shape of the music carelessly, confidently, like pulling taffy sugar, changing its colour and texture to create something all her own.

Years later, at an audition, someone asked me to sing, and I came up with the only song I knew all the way through, without needing sheet music. 'Gloomy Sunday', of course. I could sing it without even thinking.

'Holy shit, that's pure Billie,' the pianist said, taken aback. I had her artistry, parrot-fashion.

There was no ayah now, of course; the allowance from Amaryllis did not run to money for regular servants. But there were always Indians around, there were stories to be heard, things to observe, mysteries to ponder, magic to believe in. I listened and watched.

One of the guest house servants had heard of a Holy

Man due to visit the area the next day. The man could grant wishes, make things happen, he knew it for a fact.

And this could solve everything: it was a way to change our lives, to return to a safe existence, father, home, daily routine. To go to school! To learn about the things other children seemed to know about. To forget everything else.

She collects odd coins from pockets, from the top of the dressing table, from down the sides of loose-covered armchairs. She has a little ring with a red glass stone which might even be gold. Not a contribution of great value, but she is sure the Holy Man will understand.

Next morning she follows the locals, climbing a steep path out of town, up the hillside, away from the houses. She has slipped out unseen, leaving her mother asleep.

It is chilly and damp; people wear bulky jackets or shawls over saris and cotton shirts. The air drips moisture, not quite rain, but a drenching mist. She walks up the stony path, all around her the sound of dripping water as branches overloaded with moisture shed heavy globules . . . the countryside seems to be weeping.

Below them, the houses with their corrugated tin roofs are spread out along the shore of the little lake, its water today black and evil looking. Above them the higher peaks are dark, and beyond that spreads a sky of dull, even grey.

The small trickle of locals climbs on, heading for a hut tucked into the side of the hill. It is a big hut, but as they reach the doorway, Maggie sees that it is already crowded. Perhaps they are too late ('No room! No room!'). But they push in. An open fire at one end, built in the middle of the floor, glows red on a bed of stones. The smoke stings her eyes; it is stuffy, airless, with a smell of wet clothes rising like steam in the close surroundings. She is the only non-Indian, but her straight dark hair and sallow skin blend with the various shades of brown and no one pays her special attention.

The Holy Man sits by the fire and gazes placidly into the burning coals. He is squat and heavy with greasy grey hair straggling to his shoulders. He wears a black robe and some kind of animal skin slung over one shoulder. Maggie has seen a lot of Holy Men and they usually wear nothing but a tiny loincloth and a sacred thread. Sometimes they wear beads or a plain white dhoti. But this man, with his dark, ash-smeared face and eyes glowing like the coals he stirs with a stick, he is different. He must be very powerful. He will make her wish come true. The coins and the ring bite into her palm and she breathes deeply, blinking hard to keep awake. She feels faint, both from the airless heat and a fearful excitement, an awareness that this man could change it all. She must be sure to be ready when it comes to her turn. Be ready: that's the thing. She itemizes her wishes: to lead an ordinary life. To return to Amaryllis and her father and her pony. For Moti to be happy. For Maggie to go to school. That should cover everything. But suppose, for her few coins, that was asking too much. Suppose he were to say she must choose one wish. Should it be to unite the family – but that would be no good without at the same time making them happy. Should it be that then? Shaking with this terrible excitement, she knows that what she must choose is school. Please let me go to school.

She waits, pressed against the wall of the hut, watching others go up in turn, to whisper their needs, desires, their secret wishes, to the man who listens without a change of expression, accepts their offering, and gives an almost imperceptible nod. From time to time he throws a pinch of dust onto the coals, which flare up briefly into greenish flames. The air sweetens and thickens with a musky, sandalwood perfume. She has moved up, she is almost there, so close now that she can see the way his beard and grey moustaches sprout from his coarse and greasy skin. His eyes are bulbous, and the lids droop over them slowly, as though impeded by the protruding orbs.

She is next. Her hands shake as she moves towards the moment that will make her life spin and alter course. The ground seems oddly tilted so that she finds herself leaning forward as though climbing uphill.

But at the door of the hut there is a commotion: raised voices, the close-packed ranks scattering. Incredibly, it is Moti, furious, the horsy features contorted with anger and anxiety. She grabs the struggling child, without a word, and drags her away, out of the door, watched by the silent Indians.

As they stumble down the steep, stony path the child continues to struggle, crying, sobbing, screaming incoherently: 'You spoiled it all! You spoiled everything! He was just going to hear me! I would have got my wish! You spoiled it all . . .'

Moti slaps her hard, shaking her shoulders so violently that the child's teeth clatter painfully.

'*Never* do that again.' Her voice is unsteady, hoarse. 'Anything like that. The man's a charlatan. Probably dangerous. Anything could happen.'

Her voice rings in Maggie's ears. Anything could happen! Well of course it could, that was the whole point. And she has spoiled it all, storming in, bringing noise and anxiety with her. The child knows now that she will never have another chance to make everything different. She will simply have to wait. And one day when it is time, when she is old enough, she will leave. She begins to count the days. The years.

Can I really have thought that, then? Surely not. Was that not something that grew slowly, that took shape unnoticed? That day, struggling in my mother's grip, crying, despairing, I suffered in the moment; I cannot have thought ahead. I recollect suddenly that I hurled the glass ring, the coins away from me, out into the valley, to vanish down among the trees. More probably I simply thought, sobbing, that I would like to push her off the path, send her plunging down the sheer hillside after my lost offering.

But maybe it really did begin then, the counting, the waiting. I was, after all, old for my age.

Part Two

It was time to move on. I had few clothes and soon would have even fewer, for Moti had decided to do a moonlight flit. The allowance was late – or spent – and she certainly did not intend to hang on in a damp, deserted hill station until some more money arrived. We would simply walk out one morning, carrying no luggage to arouse suspicion, and we would get on a train.

What clothes I had, I wore until they fell apart – except for my best frock which I never wore. Acquired at some peak of affluence, it was made of heavy cream lace with long medieval fluted sleeves and a high neck. It had hung on padded hangers in the wardrobes of good hotels; on wire hangers in curtained corners of boarding houses; it travelled folded between tissue paper, in a trunk.

I could abandon dolls, books, polished stones and spare sandals, but to lose my best frock was inconceivable. Moti's plan was that we should wear two sets of everything we could, but lace was too precious for such treatment. I put on a cotton dress and over that a skirt and blouse and over that a cardigan. Round my neck like a bizarre scarf I gently draped the cream lace dress, and we stepped out, walking casually, not too fast, hailing a rickshaw to take us into town. Moti too, had salvaged a precious possession: the wind-up gramophone, hidden in a shopping basket.

Only when the train pulled out did I dare to approach

the window, my heart thumping with apprehension: no one was chasing us, calling out. Carefully I unwound the precious lace frock and folded it in my lap.

We moved on, from Naini with its lake, to Mussoori, to Simla, where there was a convent. I met the nuns, we bought the school uniform – Moti was always drawn to the trappings – but before term began we were on our way to somewhere new: the Allowance had just arrived and life was full of gaiety and hope. We took a longer train trip, to Delhi, bound not for a genteel guest house this time, but the Grand Hotel.

The Grand had a dining room with waiters, and a stage at one end, where a dance band played. On Friday and Saturday nights there was a cabaret. It reminded me of Russell Square and Alexander, though I did not say so.

Moti had found a dinner gown somewhere, at one of the second-hand Dress Agencies where she disappeared behind discreetly shaded windows to replenish her wardrobe. This one was almost new; green silk, it crumpled easily and would soon be marked with stains and spots and then abandoned, but for a Saturday or two it carried her triumphantly into the dining room and the dinner dance.

I knew the dining room only at breakfast time. For lunch we ate snacks bought in the bazaar and smuggled up to our room – culinary extravagance was not one of Moti's sins – but breakfast came with the room and I was instructed to take the fullest advantage of it. Consequently on Friday morning I was the last person left in the room.

The child is finishing her breakfast, cramming in a last mouthful of toast, a final scraped spoonful of papaya. Around her waiters clear tables. The lights are switched off, chandelier by chandelier, leaving the room dim and shadowy. She leaves the table, throwing down her napkin carelessly as she has been taught to: Moti says it is not done to fold your napkin neatly – it is lower class and lacks style.

She threads her way through the tables, bare now except for silver cruets and vases of flowers.

At the far end of the room, next to the stage, three young women wander listlessly in. They have curly hair and pale, unmade-up faces. They stand slackly in front of the stage while the pianist finds the music. The girls wear black fishnet stockings, black satin shorts and white blouses with full, gathered sleeves. Their high-heeled shoes clatter as they move, steel taps on the tips of the soles.

The pianist strikes the opening chords and at once a transformation takes place: back with the shoulders, on with the smile and they're off: stamp-shuffle, stamp-shuffle, stamp, stamp, stamp. Arms swinging rhythmically, taps clattering, they begin to sing to the empty room:

> *Good morning! Good mor-ning!*
> *We've danced the whole night through,*
> *Good morning, good morning, to you!*

Welcoming beams transform the tired faces; the long, beautiful legs flash and scissor. Half-hidden by a pillar the child watches the rehearsal. In the shadows she mimics the three dancers, stamp-shuffle, stamp-shuffle, tap, tap, stamp-shuffle . . . 'Good morning, good morning, to you!'

Upstairs, Moti luxuriated in the bath. We had, with dangerous recklessness, booked into a suite.

I cannot recall her talking to me much, in detail, but there are recurring images of her in her bath, an emblematic figure, *La Baigneuse*, changing subtly as the years passed; flesh that had been alabaster growing spongy, contours blurred.

Lying in her bath she contemplated her stretch marks and lamented the deterioration of her body – 'No woman's the same after childbirth. I had a particularly bad time with you, of course, thirty-six hours in labour . . . sheer agony. They gave me twilight sleep . . . useless . . .'

Then I would hear about the obstetrician, who gave her – 'Well, it was supposed to be a pain-killer, God knows what it was, bloody man stuck the needle in the wrong place . . .' She lifts her left arm, long, graceful, dripping water . . . 'No strength in the damn thing . . .' She soaps her body dreamily. 'And don't you let men handle you too much . . . look at my breasts . . . they were compared to Marie Antoinette's once. And hers were so perfect they modelled champagne goblets on them . . . before she had children, of course . . .'

Sven was one of her nicest men. He was big and burly with a loud cheerful voice, a way of laughing in sudden surprise and delight that drew humour out of others, that banished the blues.

Moti met him at some bar and he was installed in the flat by sunset. We had left the Grand – abruptly – after a scene with the management.

Being a grand hotel in tone as well as name, they were more concerned with their reputation than our money. Which was just as well. Porters carried our luggage – we had acquired some new luggage – into the marble and gilt lobby. A taxi was called.

'You will receive a cheque in due course,' Moti said haughtily.'And I intend to make an official complaint. To the Manager.' Her dress was slightly rucked up, her

80

white, high-heeled shoes grubby. The assistant manager walked away rapidly.

The flat was enormous: a cavernous sitting room, a bedroom each and one to spare. A big kitchen with antique cooking arrangements, not a serious drawback since Moti was not doing much catering.

She would thrust a few rupees into my hand and send me off to a Chinese restaurant for lunch. In retrospect it seems odd: a small child sitting in a half-empty Chinese restaurant, ordering and eating a solitary lunch, but at the time it seemed quite normal.

The reason we could afford the flat at all was its location: in old Delhi, in a once stately building in a street growing daily more disreputable. We lay, in fact, between a dubious import-export business and a brothel. No normal British family could possibly have lived there, it had been empty for years, the furniture increasingly mildewed, the fabrics rotting.

'We'll do the place up,' Moti cried, ecstatic, meaning it; 'It has real possibilities! A bit of style for once. And space!'

The wind-up gramophone was plonked, incongruously, on a vast, carved table, the music echoed hollow in the big, crumbling rooms with the vaulted ceilings, floored with old but still shining tiles.

Sven liked to dance. They went off to tea dances in New Delhi with Moti done up in a 'new' Dress Agency outfit and cobwebby American nylons. He gave me presents: boxes of chocolates, a doll with silky hair, a book of fairy tales, all of which had unhappy endings. I read the stories aloud to him and tears came to his eyes as he listened, slowly sipping his gin.

Sometimes, when they came home, they put records on the gramophone (but these must have been his, then, or did they buy them together? And what became of

81

them, later?). They danced round the big room, laughing, and steering with exaggerated care round the furniture, occasionally falling over, collapsing into an armchair. Then they vanished into the bedroom and spurts of laughter and little sounds filtered through the carved and studded door.

She cooked so rarely that I was astonished when suddenly she produced a feast, emptying shopping onto the kitchen table, crashing about with pots and pans and gulping at her glass, producing what seemed mere minutes later a soufflé, delicate vegetables, a fragrant sauce. She lit candles and stuck them on window ledges, along the tiles of the sideboard, in dishes on the big table. The lofty room glimmered with candles wavering and occasionally guttering. It smelled of hot wax and the light fell gently on her face as she raised her glass to him across the table. I see her, leaning forward a little, face slightly flushed, the room brimming with happiness, tremulous.

Sven had a wife somewhere and a family boat-building business; a life to go back to, if he got through the war. Moti sensed that he was impervious and at certain moments, when the alcohol in her system reached a critical level, she zoomed into a frenzy of resentment, trying to break him down. Usually she was able to reduce men to tears quite easily, but Sven was different.

The first time she lost her temper and hit him – once, twice, forehand, backhand across the face – he looked stunned, suddenly white faced, the marks of her fingers standing out redly.

'Apologize!' Moti snapped, eyes glassy, mouth turned down. 'Apologize, damn you!'

He shook his head. 'For what, Moti? You are now silly.'

A mistake. She began to yell, to strike his shoulders, his arms: 'Get out! Get out! And don't come back!'

He held her off, calmly. He too was a little drunk, but amiably so. He gripped her firmly, but gently, like someone preventing a child from hurting itself.

'Do not be a fool.'

She stopped struggling. Lowered her head like a bull about to charge, looking up at him balefully from under drooping lids. Murderous. He winked at her, refusing to take all the fury seriously.

And she began to laugh. To hug him, to call out for me to wind up the gramophone and put on some music, and there they were, glued together from shoulder to thigh, swaying, weaving, now fast, now slow, doing the tango on the cracked red tiles.

But the second time she hit him, he left.

We lived in Old Delhi, but our social life was New Delhi: around mid-morning we bowled along in a rickshaw, leaving the smells and market stalls, the teeming streets and noise of Chandni Chowk for Connaught Circus. Mo disappeared into a smart, dark entrance flanked by slender white columns; I crossed the road to play on the grass at the centre of Lutyens' white circus.

The child watches dogs scavenging, fighting, mating. Sometimes, urgently mounted, they lock, a muscular spasm yoking them, unwilling, together, and they become an object of amusement to passers-by. She does not laugh at the dogs; they look puzzled, harassed, uneasy.

She watches lizards flickering from wall to wall, the colour of dry earth, almost invisible in the sunlight. She watches ants working their way through the dry grass, carrying provisions, climbing painfully over obstacles – lumps of dried mud, pieces of rock, matted straw . . . one day soon the monsoon will break and without warning their parched and ordered universe will be engulfed; mass drownings will occur, earthworks and living quarters will be swept away, a world will vanish beneath the rising yellow-brown water. Meanwhile the ants work and she watches.

Everything is immaculate. Sun shines on tarmac where horse-droppings are swept up and disposed of before they cool; the white stucco gleams. The windows beneath the shady arcades are filled with cakes and European delicacies. Uniforms are everywhere and the Americans coming in on leave from building roads and air bases have money to spare. They flash rupees, chewing-gum, teeth. They are irresistibly friendly.

In Bengal there is a famine: a million people have died. In the heat of the day more and more people crowd into the shade of the arcade. Mr Gandhi – 'that bloody man' – repeatedly, patiently, implacably tells the British to 'Quit India'. She never imagines that this refers to her and Mo. This is home. And now the Japanese have entered the war and this makes things even more awkward. Mr Gandhi says the British are a 'provocation'. Will the Japanese really push through Chittagong and arrive one day in Connaught Circus? Or will it be what Mo fears: the Russians coming down through Afghanistan?

'But they're on our side –'

'So they say.'

Refugees and indigents are not supposed to clutter up the circus. But they stream in, staring blankly at the cleverly arranged heaps of fine food behind the plate glass. She watches them staring. Why do they not smash a window? March in, take possession of it all? The child moves among them, sensing no danger. Meanwhile, her mother meets a new friend. And soon another, newer friend. Maggie is introduced.

'Don't expect her to laugh at your jokes,' Moti warns;

84

'The Child is like her father, I'm afraid. Too serious. She has his nature.' She also has his brown eyes, which could be attractive, were it not for a certain flatness, a lack of sparkle, when she stares up at her mother's newest friend. She is grave and sallow, she scrutinizes and this makes some of them uncomfortable.

Moti reaches into her handbag, rummaging. From the gaping leather jaws comes a smell of stale face-powder, scent, crushed cigarettes, the metallic tang of rubbed coins. 'Take a rickshaw, darling, would you, get something to eat, I'll be home later.' She is still rummaging. Her friend has notes in a convenient pocket; he thrusts several into the child's hand.

Moti taps his arm reprovingly. 'You shouldn't . . . I'll pay you back, I don't take money from anyone . . .'

She says these things all the time, things which have nothing to do with the way they actually live: 'I'll pay you back . . . I'm getting a job soon . . . we're moving into a proper flat . . . the Child is getting a new dancing teacher . . . I don't take money –'

I certainly took money, if offered. We needed it, and besides, after paying for the rickshaw, the Chinese meal or the bottle I had been sent out to buy, there was usually some left over. This I kept.

Moti used Coty face-powder perfumed with l'Aimant, which came in a round cardboard box covered with a pattern of tiny powder puffs in apricot, white and gold. In one of these empty powder boxes I kept my hoard of rupee notes, tightly folded, annas wedged in beside them.

From time to time things arose which Moti referred to as 'contingencies'. At such times the odd savings were useful. So I was not delicate about accepting money.

When Moti wanted me out of the way for a while in London, I was pointed in the direction of St James's

Park and told to feed the ducks. In Delhi, I went to the Jantar Mantar Observatory, a maze of curving stone staircases that led nowhere, topless towers set in formal gardens; flights of wide, shallow steps, two delicate, coliseum-like structures, a circular sundial with seventy-two windows.

I did not understand the Observatory, but I was grateful for it: having Jantar Mantar available was like having the run of a giant's building-block kit all to myself – a fantastic city with all the rooms open to the sky. On most days the place was deserted. As the hours passed, the changing shadows altered the shape of the looming structures – it was a place of potent magic, mystery and a sense of melancholy. When, twenty years later, I saw a painting by de Chirico, I seemed to know his landscape already.

The child stands at the top of a twin flight of curving stairs. All around her are pillars and towers rising from the shrubs and palm trees and the dusty earth. The stone is burning hot underfoot for the morning is well advanced. The silence is broken by the noise of birds calling, complaining, pecking. These sounds only intensify the silence they invade. It is rare for Maggie's glass bell to descend on her outdoors, but today, as she stands in a sun-bleached dress of bazaar cotton, frowning at one of the massive blocks of stone, she senses the roaring un-noise beginning to envelop her; even the act of raising her head becomes an endlessly extended movement.

She is unaware of the thin, youngish Indian who has come slowly up the further flight of steps and pauses nearby. He too stares silently at the big stone triangle, standing like a vast wedge of cheese.

'You are admiring Samrat Yantra,' he says, tentatively, in English.

86

Maggie hears the voice filtered through barriers of inner space, rushing silence.

'What?'

He waves at the block enthusiastically.

'Triangle before us. Gnomon. Sundial. In the morning, shadow of gnomon falls on higher end of Western quadrant. As sun rises higher, shadow is descending till at noon there is no shadow at all. All has been calculated: altitude and azimuth. Time equals angle hour of sun.' His voice is triumphant. 'Thus, practical value of astronomical observatory.'

Maggie glances up at him and turns back to the gnomon. Time equals the angle hour of the sun? It sounds wonderful. She has no idea what it means but something is expected of her; she feels she should be polite.

'So what time is it now?' she enquires.

He consults his wristwatch with some pride: 'Eleven-fifteen precisely.'

The colonel from Chicago was not like Mo's usual friends: he was, to begin with, American. He was small and tubby and talked round a fat cigar which he ill-treated, clenching his teeth on it, mangling it, rolling it around his mouth and occasionally hurling it away. He spoke in crackling, staccato sentences, pushing his points home with his cigar, grabbing it and jabbing, stabbing at the air:

'See here, kid . . .'

It was only later, when I saw James Cagney in a film, that I realized who the colonel thought he was.

Just once, when he told her to get the goddam kid to bed, I saw Moti's eyes flash, her nostrils pinch and flare dangerously.

'*Don't* call her the goddam kid. It's *my* child and she goes to bed when *I* say so!'

87

He shrugged, grinning round the cigar, baring his teeth. 'Okay, okay, so *you* say so: you tell the kid to hit the sack.'

He stands behind her; his hands slide beneath her arms, massage her breasts confidently, expertly, pull her against him with only half-humorous urgency.

He was dynamic, the colonel. He took one look at the flat and made his announcement: 'Okay, here's what we do.'

What we did was find a new flat in a better part of town, with a kitchen that had a refrigerator and a sitting room with unmarked paintwork and freshly white-washed walls. But there was no lacy stone tracery at the windows, the ceilings were low, and there were no cracked but glowing tiles on the floor, worn smooth by the past, an invitation to the tango.

He bustled about on his short legs, chomping the cigar, and organized us. He put in furniture and said where the shiny new table and chairs should go. He carried in records: Stan Kenton, big-band jazz that rattled the crockery and blasted the walls like artillery fire. He stocked the refrigerator with food and bought drink in curiously shaped bottles – bourbon and vodka and coke.

'I drink gin,' Moti said, looking at the bottles.

'You drink too goddam much of it,' he said. 'That's another thing.'

Why did she take it? This was not like her, to be meek, to acquiesce, to agree to things. Where was the forehand-backhand, the stinging fingers, the man imploring, the goddess disdainful?

They went out and came home late, and from the bedroom came noises and movements, masculine groans and cries, exclamations, Moti's voice mumbling, gasping, but there were none of the little bursts of laughter I was accustomed to hearing at these times.

The colonel went away for a few days and at first Moti stayed in, lethargic. She looked unwell, pasty, and gloomed about, pacing the small rooms nervily. The rooms grew smaller, shrinking round us, airless. On the fourth day Mo sampled the bourbon, on the fifth the vodka and on the sixth she got dressed.

Rickshaw. Connaught Circus. Sunlight and shadow in deep stripes across the arcaded street. The grass dried up. The refugees growing more numerous. Out of the rickshaw, into the bar. Even from outside the child can hear the cries of welcome. Friends, reunion cheer: 'Moti's here!' Her back straightens, up goes the head, the scarlet mouth curls in a smile.

This time we went home together, the rickshaw speeding through the dusk, Moti swaying from side to side with the motion. Her eyes were unfocused, she saw neither the crowded street nor the lilac sky with birds wheeling black, like drops of ink, blending with the encroaching night as though the darkness were seeping out of them to spread across the last of the daylight. She laughed to herself. Thighs bumping together, elbows touching, we could have been in separate cities.

I smelled the cigar smoke as we opened the door of the flat. Mo seemed not to notice and swept in, still smiling. The colonel was standing with his back to the room, looking out of the window.

'Where were you?' he said.

(Only in films have I ever seen people stand with their backs to the room and address people. The colonel was a movie-goer.)

He swings round and looks at her. Stares at her. Begins to shout. This is the first time since they left Amaryllis that Maggie has heard anyone shout at Moti: normally *she* does the shouting, and the men capitulate, beg for forgiveness. But the colonel is definitely shouting.

What in hell is going on? he yells. The place is a mess, she's cleaned him out of liquor and on top of that –

'Lower your voice!' she raps.

He stops out of sheer surprise, but only for a moment. She must want her brains tested, he bawls, if she thinks he is going to put up with –

'Get out,' she says. 'Out, out, *out!*'

The child remains by the door, watching. For a moment the two voices battle, rising to a crescendo.

'You dreadful little man –'

' – you bitch! –'

' – go back where you –'

' – now hear *this* –'

Then her mother acts. Two strides across the room – it is a small room, after all – and she is within striking distance. She is taller than the colonel and in her high heels she stares down at him coldly, a basilisk, deadly. Her arm swings: forehand-backhand, crack! crack! The colonel's face snaps left and right, comically, but the colonel is not laughing. Nor is he falling to his knees, begging forgiveness, nor is he crying. The colonel is a man of action.

His left hand smashes her across the head; a right to her jaw knocks her against the wall. She begins to slide towards the floor, dazed, blood trickling from her mouth, but he has by no means finished. He drags her upright by both shoulders and slams her on the side of her head. He hits her again. And again. Then he lets her drop.

The child, frozen by the door, is suddenly freed from her paralysis. She throws herself across the prostrate woman, crying, trying without success to raise her up.

Behind them, the colonel flexes sore knuckles and advises the bitch to get her ass off the floor and clean the place up before he comes back. He pays the rent, he reminds her. He wants to see it looking good. To encourage her he empties an overflowing ashtray onto the floor and stomps out, making sure he bangs the door.

Moti lies curled up, huddled against the wall, hands clasped over her head to ward off any further blows. Never before has Maggie seen her defenceless, defeated. She smooths her mother's hair, crying, comforting. Slowly Moti sits up, ungainly, bruises already visible against the white flesh.

She patted my head almost absently. There was blood on her mouth and when she spoke the split flesh oozed blood which hung, viscous and trembling on her lip till it overflowed suddenly down her chin.

'Foolish little man,' she mumbled. Did he not realize, with his pot-belly, his unattractive face, his ghastly table-manners, how incredibly lucky he was to have enjoyed her company for even one hour?

'He blew his nose on his table napkin, you know.'

It was the first time that, for material comfort, she had taken on a man she neither pitied nor was attracted to. Now she could see how unwise this had been.

'One must not lower one's standards.'

She reached out, wincing, her movements cautious, and drew me closer to her.

'I'm afraid this has all been rather a mistake, darling.' She pulled up her skirt hem and wiped the blood off her chin. 'I think we have time to pack a few things.'

Hastily they pack, throwing clothes into suitcases, running every few seconds to the window to check for any sign of the colonel. Then they are ready, Mo's skirt bloodstained, Maggie's face streaked with dirty tears.

'Wash your face,' Moti says.

91

'Change your skirt,' Maggie advises. Moti looks down at herself and shrugs impatiently.

'I'll say we were caught in a riot.' They laugh, pushing the suitcases through the door, bumping them down the stairs.

'I did it for you,' Moti says. 'I wanted you to have a nice room of your own, a decent place.'

Did she really believe that? Probably not: it was simply the right sort of thing to say, like 'I pay my way' and 'The Child needs a new dancing teacher.' But I believed it, I felt guilty. For my sake she had been beaten to the ground by a monster. If only a Holy Man were around, if only magic could be summoned up to help, to destroy the colonel. Poisoned bourbon. An exploding cigar. A krait in his bed. A scorpion in his shoe. If only.

When Georges Clemenceau visited the not-quite-finished New Delhi in 1931 he is said to have remarked, 'What handsome ruins it will make!' And so it will, one day. Those columns, those arcaded streets, that graceful circus, the imperial architecture – one sees it crumbling already.

I went back, a long time afterwards. I walked down Rajpath that had been called Kingsway, round Connaught Circus, and the smooth white stucco had flaked and fallen, there were raw places and gaps and sagging lintels.

Slowly, issuing from tiny fissures here and there, the creepers and wild grass so picturesque in Piranesi will spread, growing stronger, widening the cracks that house them, festooning the dying city, decorating while they destroy.

But I remember it still as a gleaming place, white columns, sparkling mansions; an architect's dream that for once looked as good on the ground as on the drawing board. I remember how hard it was to accept Moti's decision: time to move on.

Time to move on. At the station Mo reacted nervily to every distant figure in US Army drab. The colonel had turned out to be surprisingly vindictive, causing scenes, threatening to report her – to whom and for what I never knew, but that was when she made the decision: head for a new city. It was, after all, a pattern.

At the station we paced the platform, waiting for departure time; it was late, territory had already been taken over for the night, people establishing individual claims to small portions. Men, women, children, wrapped tightly in thin cloth coverings, lay stretched out, straight legged, sleeping; heads and faces covered, feet sticking out like brown twigs. In their white shrouds they looked like corpses and lay as unmoving, while we stepped over and between them, picking our way to the train.

Porters in red tunics, balancing trunks and cases on their heads, moved at a rolling trot; unerringly finding with their bare feet the few inches of platform left free between bodies; nobody tripped, nobody stirred.

Mo looked cheerful. Moving on always carried an element of hope in it: a new city, new people. Perhaps she would find something interesting to do; meet someone amusing and kind. Adventures of every sort lurked, waiting to be discovered. Perhaps our lives would be changed.

And our lives were indeed about to be changed. But not just yet. First the journey, days and nights of delight, rocked to sleep by the train, hearing the slop-slop of water in the zinc tub on the compartment floor as the huge block of ice slowly melted; the sound of the engine whistle shrilling through the darkness, the clanking bell as we approached a wayside station, slowing, gliding past dark platforms neatly stacked with sleeping forms, their winding-sheets ghostly white against the smoky blackness.

Just before dawn I woke to see the grey landscape slowly turning to rose. An occasional cow or buffalo standing in a field lifted its head as we passed; a man squatted, defecating by the railway. The sun rose slowly over the horizon, soft, glowing, a deep, carmine pink. For a few moments the landscape lay bathed in this gentle, rosy radiance. Then suddenly the sun was high, everything beneath it bleached and still.

*　　*　　*

We moved on. From Delhi to Agra; the Hindus said that somewhere between the two, Krishna was born, the eighth avatar of Vishnu. Sometimes I paused at one of the shrines to put in a word: Vishnu the preserver, please preserve us. (Meanwhile at bed-time I hedged the bet: Gentle Jesus, meek and mild . . .)

We came to Benares, heading for Calcutta, like pilgrims following the course of the Jumna to the mouth of the Ganges.

It was a precarious journey, depending always on the arrival of the next allowance from Amaryllis, the poste restante our lifeline. She made no plans; we drifted. I see now that there must have been fear there, kept at bay: one slip too far, one incident too messy and we could have plunged from the tightrope of the merely disreputable into the abyss. She used her men, but only to a point. We maintained – just – our independent status. Lentil soup and potatoes for supper frequently, smart bars when possible. And always, of course, First Class on the train. Everything was perfect on the train. Could that be why those long journeys, whole days and nights of them, were highlights?

94

Those places we stopped at, I recall nothing about them. Benares was the place for gold-encrusted silk, they said, but I saw none. Agra I went back to, later, so that I too could nod, gazing at the Taj Mahal, and say yes, it is all they say. At the time I took it for granted, like so much else.

Another mosque. Another temple. Another city. How was I to know that all the while I should have been saying to myself, look hard. Retain. This is special. Remember this. What I recall are the sheets. On Moti's bed the sheets were never white, blank, but marbled like the end-papers in an old book with swirls of subtle colour: a blend of semen and spilt tea, whisky and menstrual blood, hair-oil and face powder. Sometimes there were buttery crumbs from breakfast in bed, or a nacreous fleck or two from a sardine midnight feast. Occasionally there were objects – a bottle top, a coin, a hairpin, but always there were the stains, forming a sort of biography of those who occupied the bed.

In Calcutta there was no white Lutyens circus; no co-siness of scale, none of the contained quality of New Delhi, nor the defined bustle of Chandni Chowk in the old town. Calcutta stretched out vast, shapeless, hopeless. Howrah Station was a bedlam; the Hooghly as we drove over the bridge was already lined with people washing, praying, cleaning utensils, filling brass water pots. Bodies and water gleamed in the morning light. Further out, in mid-stream, things bobbed on the surface, drifted with the current: excrement, dead animals, rotting vegetation, half-decomposed corpses of those too poor to use the burning ghats.

Our battered taxi had two men in the front seats: Sikhs, bearded, turbanned and fierce looking. Our head bearer at Amaryllis had looked like this and he was gentle as an ayah. The man next to the driver caught my eye.

'First time in Calcutta, missy?'

Moti chose to ignore the question. I nodded.

'Yes. Well I was born here, but I don't remem—'

Moti touched my sandal with her shoe. I stopped.

When we got out they remained in their seats, not helping unload our cases. This surprised me, but should not have: 'Quit India', 'Swaraj', 'British Go Home', we had already seen the slogans daubed on walls.

A passing Englishman, elderly, leather faced, paused and helped Moti lift a suitcase from the taxi. Quietly he said, 'Forgive me, not a good idea, two drivers . . . kick one out before you get in. They won't argue. They know it's against the law.'

She looked surprised. 'I never have trouble with natives. They're all right if you treat them decently.'

We went through the gates and up a curving drive overshadowed with trees and undergrowth burgeoning out of control. Through a tunnel of jungle greenery I saw the house.

We had moved down in the world, to an Armenian boarding house, a family affair in a rambling warren of dark corridors and large, damp rooms leading onto verandas and a shady garden full of trees which grew thick and tall, pressing up against the walls of the house. Monkeys sat in the trees and watched and chattered noisily, but not as noisily as the Alkazarians.

They were a complex family, including not only Mr and Mrs A. but aunts and cousins, a couple of daughters and several uncategorized old people who sat about in corners all day and were seen on their feet only at meal times, tottering towards the dining room.

The boarding house was cheap. It was also noisy. None of the Alkazarians spoke, they shouted: Mr A. shouted at Mrs. She shouted at the servants; they both shouted at the guests, most of whom (being in some complicated way related) shouted back.

They had infinitely varied ways of shouting. Mr Alkazarian, well fleshed and virile in shirtsleeves and baggy trousers, bawled for his breakfast, flinging back his head and shaking his grey curls impatiently.

This was a sort of wake-up call to the rest of us. Mrs A. then screamed at the cook who began to make clattering noises in the kitchen next to the house. Mrs Alkazarian was as big as her husband and seemed always to wear the same print frock, with flip-flop sandals on her feet. They looked rumpled; their skin, which had a jaundiced glow, was shiny with perspiration even before the heat of the day. Both of them were vigorous, barely able to contain their energy. Even at their loudest, most enraged pitch of vocal extravagance they never looked angry: they thrived on the shouting and perhaps it took the place of exercise for I never saw either of them leave the house.

We all ate together in the dining room, most people seated at the big family table in the middle of the room, squeezed up, rubbing chairs, reaching across each other for thick Armenian bread, olives, pickles. Evey meal began with tall green glasses of ice-cold water melon cut in cubes and left to steep so that the glass was half filled with sweet liquid from the fruit. You spooned out the water melon, then drank the fresh syrup. Mr Alkazarian gobbled the water melon quickly, slapping his lips and making noises of satisfaction, then he slurped the liquid down. Moti flinched, delicately stirring her melon around with the long, slender spoon that reached down to the bottom of the glass.

She hated the big table, the pushing, the noise. She hated what she called the dreadful mediocrity of it all. She yearned for white, starched tablecloths, waiters with silver tongs placing crisp rolls on side plates, pouring

97

wine. There should be music from a dance band on the dais, muted conversation from adjoining tables placed well apart; chandeliers glimmering overhead, sports cars, the opera.

But she had no inkling of the magic that the Alkazarians possessed: they had photo-albums with worn leather covers and blunted corners full of sepia prints of people in funny clothes seated stiffly in hard chairs or holding horses' bridles against backgrounds of strange, wild landscape. There was a wedding photograph with a small, richly dressed bride hung about with jewels, her face framed in a lace head-dress. It reminded me of that wedding attended long ago, the girl with silver tears painted on her cheeks, pearls threaded in her hair.

They had silver ornaments and little boxes painted in bright colours that cluttered every shelf and surface. There were knives in carved scabbards, crunchy velvet tablecloths with fringes and candlesticks of beaten silver.

They told stories in oddly accented, inaccurate English about an old country; of terrible events concerning Sultans and Bolsheviks, Turks and territory, a policy of extermination – a phrase I was to hear again, later.

'Seven thousand they killed in Constantinople, in just two days. That was 1896 –'

'Seven thousand? What are you talking? Eight *hundred* thousand, that's what *I* know. Extermination, no?'

They, like us, were not *of* India, but simply *in* India. I had only recently become aware of the difference. Mr Gandhi said that if the British were to leave India, the Japanese would not attack. Our presence was 'a provocation'. Not home after all, then. But for us there was always England to go back to, if necessary. The Alkazarians were Armenians. They had nowhere.

*

98

Mrs Alkazarian passes plates down the table, heaped with lamb and steaming vegetables. The old people eat slowly, dribbling gravy.

When the Alkazarians find the child alone – 'That mother of yours gone off again, has she?' – they give her bananas; they pat her shoulder and pinch her cheeks and shout at each other over her head. She is drawn into the kitchen, like a tiny boat swept into the wake of two bustling tugs. The house is filled with noise and movement so that the child ceases to wait, apprehensively, for the humming, crushing weight of solitary silence, the roar of un-noise, the glass bell sealing her off.

Instead, when Mo goes out, the Alkazarians call out to Maggie to come on in, see what we've got here, then, and they hand her sticky cakes and fudge wrapped in shiny paper. 'Nice, eh?' they shout. 'Try one of these, nuts and honey, lovely.' Their voices bang round the room, bouncing into corners and shaking the woodwork, banishing silence.

All this was fortunate because soon Mo was out a lot and I was left to my own devices. She had found a job, a real job, not fantasy. A real job with a salary, but better than that, a uniform!

She had washed, dressed carefully and avoided the bars en route. She arrived on time for an appointment with a group of people who were taking on British women to do work 'of a sensitive nature'. Mo spoke beautifully, she had an authoritative manner, alert eyes and she looked intelligent. No wonder they were fooled. In fact, when sober she *was* intelligent. The problem was she had a part-time brain and this was a full-time job.

She appreciated the money, but she really adored the uniform: khaki drill bush jacket and trousers. She took it to a bazaar tailor and had him alter it to fit rather better than regulations intended: the jacket now outlined her small bosom to advantage, the trousers hugged her trim bottom. She acquired a snappy leather shoulder bag. With her height and long legs she looked rakish and attractive and at the same time efficient.

The job was to do with plotting the positions of aircraft, and the way Moti told it, she and the other plotters were key figures in military intelligence, stationed in Flight Operations, ensuring the minute-by-minute accuracy of a huge table-top map on which the movements of planes were charted.

For a while she arrived on time. Then she was a little late, then very late. One day she failed to show up at all. This I was unaware of, left behind at casa Alkazarian. She still went off each day in her uniform, though not always at the same hour: 'Shift-work, darling, well there's a war on, you have to pitch in . . .'

Two weeks later an enquiry came through from the Operations Room: was she unwell? Please report.

Somehow it became difficult for her to go back, awkward really. 'Anyway it's bloody boring work, just standing around on one's feet pushing model planes about on a map with those damn fool sticks like garden rakes . . . hardly requires intelligence and initiative, glorified clerks, really. I'm going to tell them to sod off.'

She told them nothing, but she held onto the uniform. She should probably have been arrested, but nothing happened and she wore it for weeks, cutting quite a dash with new acquaintances – 'Intelligence work, mmm, can't say more, I'm afraid . . .' – until the uniform grew grubby and creased, and by then the jacket was growing a little tight around the middle so one day she threw it into the bottom of the wardrobe and forgot about it.

I have no recollection of her telling me, but soon I knew that she was pregnant. How long had she known?

100

Was that perhaps why she had accepted the colonel's proposition? Security, for a while, under such circumstances, might have had an allure.

At first she tried to ignore it; perhaps if she closed her eyes it would go away. But it did not go away. She drank a lot of gin, took hot baths and bought tablets. But it remained, so she shrugged and went in search of new friends. Life continued. Time passed, shaping itself into a nine-month funnel. She managed to make me feel guilty even about my style of arrival: 'Of course I had the best when you were born . . . leading gynaecologist, excellent man, he'd been called in by the Royal Family earlier on . . . Obstetrician by Appointment . . .' The new arrival, she implied, would probably be born on the pavement.

But all that was not for ages yet. On with the face and the frock and the dance.

The Alkazarians were suggesting that some rent could be paid. They shouted, waving their arms, and insisted that the bill must be settled – at least in part – by the end of the week.

Moti decided it would be simpler if we moved on.

'Do we have to? I like it here.'

'You *like* it? But they're dreadful. Quite impossible.'

'But they're friendly –'

'Oh, they're *friendly*. Armenians are always *friendly*.'

This was when she said she knew Michael Arlen, who wrote *The Green Hat*. 'An overpraised book in my opinion, he had absolutely no understanding of the sort of woman he was writing about, all that stuff about the pagan body in the Chislehurst mind – *Chislehurst* – I ask you!' She said he thought like a foreigner. 'I met him once, at the theatre, and the very next night I found he was sitting next to me at dinner. Of course his name wasn't really Arlen at all, nor Michael either. It was Dickran something, a Turkish Delight sort of name – Loukhoumades, something like that. He was very much the English gentleman, let me know he was educated at Public School – a minor one . . . Malvern, I think, and he was part of the Riviera set of course –'

'He doesn't sound much like Mr and Mrs Alkazarian –'

'If you go back far enough you'll find they have something in common, Bulgaria, Azerbaijan, Lithuania –'

Lithuania? Lithuania. The *Luftwaffe* pilot in Russell Square pushes away his breakfast: 'You bring me an egg from *Lithuania*, maybe from a *Jewish* chicken!'

Armenia, Lithuania, extermination. It seemed there were connections between these things.

Mo was talking on. '. . . One day he stopped writing, somebody told me he listed his profession in his passport as Retired Writer . . .'

He sounded like a figure of mystery and sadness, Michael Arlen, but to Mo he was just another Armenian.

Anyway, we were doing another flit and this time it would be easier because she had found a flat not far away and she could smuggle out a few things at a time: the gramophone first.

On the final trip we put on our extra layers as usual and stepped out confidently – or rather Mo stepped out confidently, I followed at her heels, heart thumping. And this time with reason: Mr Alkazarian stood waiting on the front veranda, arms crossed.

'I thank you to wait a minute –'

Moti pauses, up goes the head, eyes flash, nostrils pinch and flare dangerously.

'About the rent –

She grimaces. 'You'll get the rent –'

He nods. 'I'm sure. Meantime you can leave this extra

stuff you've got there, take off this extra stuff, please –'

The child complies at once, pulling the spare frock over her head, handing him the cardigan. The ivory lace dress she holds on to, rolled into a ball in her hand, hoping it will not be noticed. Her mother pauses, then quite casually unbuttons her loose jacket and throws it disdainfully at Alkazarian. He eyes her bulky shape.

'What's that under your blouse?'

She gives him a look of seraphic grace and pulls up her blouse: clearly visible, her naked belly bulges, swelled to solid roundness. He looks astounded, shocked, dismayed. Suddenly he thrusts the clothes back at us.

'Here, take this stuff, just go now!' He turns quickly into the house.

As the woman and the child go down the steps of the veranda, clutching bundles of clothing, he reappears and shouts after them.

'Kid! Here a minute!'

She climbs the veranda steps and looks up at the big, bulky man. He thrusts a banana into her hand and pinches her cheek, hard.

She hurries down the drive to the street. She is hungry. At the Alkazarians' they will soon be sitting down to lunch. She peels the banana and takes a bite.

O sad, pathetic figure. The little one, trailing after the unmindful adult. These bids for sympathy, these plangent statements. Weren't there moments of closeness, of adventure, of discovery? Surely there were moments: the songs she sang. And what about the laughs?

Now, without looking back, she calls over her shoulder, 'We'll have a nice supper. I'll make some lovely lentil soup and potatoes.'

Disloyally I think of the big table at the Alkazarians', of the lamb so tender it falls off the bone, of the desserts sticky with honey. (And all that week we eat lovely lentil soup and potatoes; the allowance is clearly late.)

'I've got a banana Mr Alkazarian gave me.'

'Have you?' A glance back over her shoulder. '*Must* you eat in the street?'

The child chews another mouthful. The woman slows down, shrugs.

'All right, beast, I'll have a bite. Just a small one.'

Moti was going dancing. She hurried into her clothes, choosing one of her looser frocks – short skirted, square shouldered. She studied herself in a worn and scratched mirror screwed to the wall, then pulled up her skirt, dragged on a greyish stretch-panty and pulled down the frock. She nodded, satisfied.

'Hardly shows,' she said firmly.

She looked well: pregnancy agreed with her, and her skin, which sometimes took on a finely puckered, dry appearance, was smooth and glowing like the alabaster eggs in the bazaar. Her arthritis was growing worse; she found the pain hard to take sometimes but gave no sign of this to outsiders. Friends were for fun, for laughing, for telling endless variations on long, involved and faintly *risqué* stories –

'And Little Audrey laughed and laughed, because she knew *exactly* where the toadstool was . . .'

One of the people who laughed with Moti was a river-pilot called Ruddy, a small, sharp-eyed man with a bushy beard. He would appear suddenly at the end of a spell of night duty and be roaring with Moti before the hour was out – 'Gin and tonic before breakfast, best way to start the ruddy day!' She had given him his nickname as a tribute to his limited vocabulary: 'ruddy difficult bit of water this morning . . . ruddy good little runner, that pony . . .'

104

Ruddy was a Hooghly pilot, the aristocracy of the species: Conrad and Kipling wrote complimentary things about Hooghly pilots, he told us, and they were paid more – practical proof that the Hooghly was more difficult than other rivers.

Uncannily skilled, Hooghly pilots guided ships safely through the treacherous, shifting sandbanks, seemingly sniffing out navigation channels which altered unpredictably with the tide. They basked in public admiration and lived well: Ruddy owned racehorses and a Bugatti.

What remains of him is the way he had of making simple events seem extraordinary.

'Swimming,' he anounced, arriving one morning. 'Got the motor outside.'

We drove beyond the city, following the river whose perverse ways he had mastered, while Ruddy waved his arms alarmingly, letting go of the steering wheel to do so, shouting mysterious explanations.

'Over that way, see, Hooghly Point, river swings to the right when you're coming in, just *there*. As we're making our approach, her port bow catches the current. Your starboard's being pushed up-river by the flood tide, while your ruddy port bow's met head-on. You have to watch yourself.'

It was the trickiest ribbon of water in the world: the river twisted and turned, it rose and fell at speed. There were places where if the pilot got it wrong by even a few inches he could send the ship spinning onto a shoal of quicksand that would suck it down and swallow it whole. It happened, he told us, in the past: the shifting sands were rich with the ingested wrecks of lost ships. And now? Could it happen now? Ruddy laughed. 'Not with me. The ruddy Hooghly won't get *me*, never fear.'

Past the shoe factory and the brick works we came to the jute mills and beyond them to trees packed close like jungle. Here the jute grew, stems and bark which would be gathered and processed to become gunny sacks and rope so rough that, handled carelessly, it burnt the hands or filled the fingertips with tiny fibre splinters.

Ruddy was embarking on another of his explanations: 'You'll find retting pools all round here, for soaking the fibres so that they can –'

Moti interrupted him, her voice sharp. 'Anyone from Dundee knows about jute, for God's sake, Ruddy.' Her mouth curved downwards. He looked surprised at the tone and went quiet.

After a moment she relented, patting his hand. 'Not your fault.'

On that brief visit 'home' to Moti's brother, I had seen the old photographs, the men in high collars and curious hats posed stiffly in front of a tall black building. Moti's grandfather was one of the mill-owners who turned over their machines to jute when the nineteenth-century boom was on. Then someone took out a machine to Bengal and sold it and got orders for more. The trade flourished; they grew unexpectedly rich. Later her grandfather – and others – regretted that mushrooming export of machinery, when the Bengalis elbowed the Scots out of the competition and the Dundee market died.

'All very sad,' Moti said briskly; but in any case by then her father was on the way to becoming the eminent architect, and machinery and jute were treated as a shadowy area of the family's past.

We drove on through the green tangled undergrowth, then left the car and walked, till suddenly we came upon an oblong of blue, milky water completely surrounded by trees: the trees grew close together, stem nudging stem, and came almost to the water's edge, like walls. The blue sky seemed to press the hot air down on top of us like a lid; we were boxed in by the trees and the sky.

*

106

There is a smell of green heat; a moist, heavy presence. All over her body the pores of her skin prickle open, there are tiny movements around her: plant tendrils reach imperceptibly towards a new support; seed pods crack, petals gape wider, shoots push free of the earth . . .

Surely this turquoise clearing in the green density cannot be one of the tanks where jute is washed? Perhaps it is, perhaps it is simply a tank of ordinary water for industrial use.

To the child it is a place of new magic: the trees slim as spears, more green, more tightly packed than real trees, the leaves juicier; the water, heated by the sun to a silver shimmer unlike any other pool, a blue-white milkiness that is almost viscous.

Between the trees and the water there is a narrow shelf, a sort of no-man's land where clothes are shed and picnic baskets parked in the shade. Jumping, diving, splashing, they laugh; there are shrieks of pleasure that startle the birds so that they rise flapping out of the trees. From the depths of the green shadows unseen eyes watch the trio cavorting like savages by the water's edge.

Once, in England, we went to Droitwich spa. The brine springs, the 'wyches', are mentioned in the Domesday Book, and we were there to try and help Moti's arthritis. I have a memory, a puzzling vision, of watching her and other women in a sort of swimming pool, up to their necks in water, on which floats a small tray set with cups from which they sip. Could this have been a cure? Now on the opalescent water in the clearing, Mo floats on her back. On her belly, breaking the surface like a turtle's shell, she rests a bakelite cup of gin and tonic. Everyone laughs.

*

When the laughter died away, silence returned to the clearing, sleepy, still, intensified by the occasional buzz of an insect, the plop of a bubble bursting on the blue-white surface.

We lay, gasping with heat beneath the trees and slept and woke dazed, emptied, to drive back slowly into the city.

We lived in one room which served as bedroom as well as living room. There was a kitchen of sorts and a bathroom but no refinements. Furniture was sparse. It was a room to sleep in. During the day Mo spent her happiest hours in Firpo's, which called itself a restaurant, though she never ate there. Firpo's was smart, a finger-hold on the world of respectability, and she chose her clothes carefully when she went there.

Her mother has a system for dressing: all the clothes she owns are thrust into the wardrobe on arrival at a new place. Some are hung up, most lie heaped at the bottom. Each day when the time comes to get dressed she picks over the heap and chooses the least soiled, least crumpled items.

She hums one of her favourite songs, *'I'm off with the Wraggle-Taggle Gypsies-O'*, or, more often,

Keep away from bootleg hooch, when you're on the spree;
Take, good, care of yourself, you belong to me . . .

When there are no servants (and these days there are usually no servants) no washing is done. The clothes get dirtier and the choice more limited, but at least no time is wasted in dreary manual labour. Like the Mad Hatter's tea party, when one lot is used up, move on.

Finally she wails, 'I haven't a thing to wear!' then she goes to a Dress Agency with discreet, curtained

108

windows, and buys something nearly new. In the bottom of the wardrobe the pile grows larger.

Maggie has fewer clothes, usually two dresses and some knickers, now rather small for her. She takes a rupee or two, goes into the market and buys cheap, printed cotton. At another stall, further down the street, a man with a sewing machine, Mr Gupta, runs up a dress for her in half an hour, copying a picture she has torn out of an old magazine.

The dress can be rinsed out and hung in the bathroom to dry overnight, but village cotton has its dangers: cold-water wash only is one of the rules. Today she has forgotten this and shakes the bar of soap about in hot water, frothing up bubbles. In with the dress and – horrors, she snatches it out, watches it shrinking ('shutting up like a telescope', yes Alice) and hastily turns on the cold tap before it disappears altogether. Too late. She stares at a handkerchief-sized garment. Money will have to be wasted, having another run up without delay.

Mr Gupta is busy: 'Come back in two hours, I have a gentleman's outfit to complete. Formal wear.'

She wanders further in the bazaar, sniffing sweetmeats, fried potato puffs, spices, drains. The smoke from evil-smelling bidi cigarettes drifts past her.

A man is being shaved at one stall; at another, a scribe is writing a letter for a worried illiterate. Columns of glass bangles, red, yellow, green; beads tiny as seeds strung into necklaces; silver anklets, herbal cures, fruit, star-apples piled in a yellow heap . . . (a wedding, a star-apple tree in the garden, the swing festooned with jasmine . . .).

The crowd pushes past pale, velvety cows with black-ringed eyes placidly munching from vegetable stalls; stray dogs and legless beggars occupy the pavements splotched with the crimson sputum of the betel-nut chewers.

Chowringhee, where her mother has vanished into the cool, dark comfort of Firpo's, adjoins the huge green expanse of the Maidan. She sits under the shade of a tree and watches the pie-dogs. People talk to her. Then it is time to go back to the bazaar, to get her dress made.

'This was an area of swampland, pestilence ridden,' Mr Gupta says, biting off a thread. 'People went in fear of tigers. Now it is a bad place still. Goondas, politicals . . . I suppose you belong to the Calcutta Turf Club?' he enquires hopefully.

She has never heard of the Calcutta Turf Club and can see he is disappointed. He sits cross legged at his machine on the floor of the little shop, completes the final seam, turns the dress right side out and hands it to her.

At night the pavements are covered with sleeping bodies, tightly packed as on the platforms of the railway stations. The lights of the smart restaurants and shops spill out onto pavements littered with debris and humanity without hope.

And in one of these smart places, where the cocktail shakers are busy and the American dance band tunes are up to date, Moti suddenly stops in mid fox-trot and begins to walk, awkwardly and urgently, from the dance floor.

Hospital. Strange that I had never been inside a hospital – not since that first time, when indeed I came *out* rather than went in. Hospital smelt peculiar, and echoed like some of the old temples: footsteps and voices were hollow and people looked serious.

She was doing well, very well, the Anglo-Indian nurse said cheerfully, and so was the baby – 'My, what a speedy one, eh? We got her in here just in time. Your daddy looked very relieved.'

My *daddy*? Surely not. He could hardly have got here

110

from Amaryllis already. Some mystery to be unravelled. I said nothing. It was often best to remain wooden when puzzled or alarmed.

In the hospital bed she looked even paler than usual – almost blue beneath her skin – but jubilant.

'Amazing, darling. At ten o'clock I was actually dancing. And an hour and a half later, all over. Amazing. When I think of the time I had with you, thirty-six hours in labour . . .'

Maggie glances about, looking for the baby. The speed of delivery does not startle her: dogs, goats, cows, they seem to have their young quite swiftly. But where is it? And what is it? Boy or girl?

Hovering at the door now, behind her, a very tall man with scarred cheeks, sweating slightly, touching his moustache with his middle finger as though to reassure himself it still exists, seems uncertain whether he should intrude. Moti waves him in gaily.

'There you are! This is Margaret-Rose, my daughter.' She turns to me, 'I simply do not know what I'd have done without Shorty –' *Shorty?* – 'Maggie, this is Shorty, who probably saved my life.'

He sweats with embarrassment, his eyes are dog-like. He is a sergeant in the Guards.

Normally Mo would not have been dancing with a sergeant; on the whole she kept to the officer class. But the evening had been lively; she was in a particularly benevolent mood and the tall young sergeant with acne scars on cheeks and brow looked lonely. She decided to be magnanimous.

'Your mother has a wonderful smile,' Shorty muttered, apparently addressing the back of the rickshaw wallah patiently jogging between the shafts. He had, of course, insisted on seeing me home safely.

111

'She's eight,' Mo had told him earlier, patting my shoulder maternally. I was nine, going on ten, and quite used to taking myself wherever I needed to go.

The rickshaw trundled lightly over potholes and debris, swerving every few minutes to avoid head-on collisions. Shorty continued to detail my mother's virtues. I pieced it together very quickly: wonderful smile : . . shy young sergeant . . . would she care to dance? . . . brave, beautiful woman . . . on her own with a child (she might have decided to be a widow, that evening).

And dancing, talking, rather enjoying the rare treat of a tall man, of being able to look *up* at a dancing partner, Moti suddenly feeling various disturbing and disagreeable sensations that heralded baby.

Some men might have melted into the crowd. Others might have panicked, or simply put her into a cab.

'Shorty was wonderful,'she said, glowing. 'He organized everything.'

Shorty got her to hospital, paid for the private room, and next day appeared with toys, lacy bed-jacket, baby clothes and a cradle for the brother I now had. She took all this, graciously, as her right. And so did he.

He moved us out of the seedy room into a flat; he cooked, cleaned, washed clothes – somewhere he had actually found, and now donned, an apron. I would have sworn Mo did not possess one.

Shorty loved her. He was devoted and selfless and brought out the worst in her. I heard him crying one night and unwisely peered through my bedroom door: he was on his knees, attempting to kiss her feet. She tried, half-heartedly, to kick him away, and when he raised his head imploringly, she slapped his face – forehand, backhand, crack, crack, but there was no great force behind the blows.

'Oh get *up*,' she snapped, 'for Christ's sake get off your knees.' He simply went on crying, begging for –

112

what? I never knew. A moment later the door banged and she was gone. Suffocated by the mediocrity of existence in the flat, the unbearable weight of her sergeant's affection, she had gone out in search of fresh air and real life.

Shorty changed the baby. I watched: I examined the small, wrinkled body, the legs kicking and straightening like a frog's. The blue, beady eyes, the bright ginger hair. I had asked her once, earlier on, who the father was and she had been evasive, but there was no doubt now: baby was the product of that afternoon at the hill station guest house, the tea-tray forgotten, sheets twisted, the spent member nesting in the bright pubic bush.

Baby had creases at neck and groin, almost like an old man, but he had a tiny, smooth, perfect penis, a bud, unmarked, and Shorty and I knelt and adored him, an inadequate duo of Magi.

Shorty was away for a few days. I had learned to prepare the baby-feed, sterilize the bottles and rubber teats – 'Poor little mite,' Moti remarked, glancing at him dispassionately, 'I breast-fed you for months. I had masses of milk then . . .'

She made up her face, selected a cleanish frock and went out. She was delighted by Shorty's absence: his dependence increasingly irritated her. He clung. He begged. She spurned.

Moti preferred to ignore birthdays – her own as well as mine – above all this particular birthday when I was edging into double figures, though no one would know that – 'Yes, a big girl for nine, well, she was a bonny Scottish baby . . .' Shorty, however, had found out about it and left a cardboard box to be opened on the day.

*

The box is mysterious: gleaming, stippled silver card-board. Too small to be a shoe-box, and the wrong shape. Quite heavy. Shaken, it gives out no tell-tale rattle of chocolates or sweetmeats. What then? A doll? A very small, heavy doll it would have to be. Building bricks then?

At last she lifts the lid. Beneath a layer of white tissue paper the box contains a small book bound in soft black leather. The Holy Bible. Its pages are fragile, gold edged, and there are illustrations: the coat of many colours, the Burning Bush, the entry into Jerusalem, the Crucifixion . . .

On the flyleaf are two words, written in black ink with a thick nib: *'and Shorty'*. The child is puzzled. An odd thing to write in a book. But the Bible is beautiful, filled with poetry and magic of a new kind. She reads it every day.

In a small English church five years later, when I knelt for the laying on of hands at Confirmation and heard no beat of doves' wings above my head, felt no divine fire, it was Shorty's bible I held. By then I had worked out the flyleaf mystery: dear, kind, abject Shorty, leaving space for Moti to compose something suitable and add her name. How could he know she hated writing any-thing, even messages in birthday books?

He was still away when we had a visitor a few days later: a stranger in uniform, with the three crowns of a captain on his epaulettes. He stood outside the door of the flat in khaki shorts and bush jacket, looking very young but at the same time important, tapping his shorts with his swagger-stick. He requested permission to come in, seemed embarrassed: delicate matter, hoped she wouldn't . . .

He had come to ask her to stop seeing Shorty. I

listened from the next room, missing words, but I got the gist. 'For his own good . . . needs the money for his mother in England . . . army career to consider . . .'

He left quite soon, and when a little later the baby began to cry, Mo wound up the gramophone with vicious energy, poured a large gin and played 'Gloomy Sunday' a few times. She looked round the room with dissatisfaction. The signs were clear.

Perhaps this time we moved on for the right reasons: because it was best for someone else. Perhaps she saw it as a Marguerite Gautier gesture: noble and self-sacrificing, even heroic. And perhaps it really was. Or was it simply that she was bored?

The allowance must have arrived about then for she bought herself a new blue dress and a small, tip-tilted hat with a tiny veil. It made her long nose and now rather haggard face look elegant and almost beautiful again. Staring into the mirror at her gleaming image, I suddenly saw how much she had changed.

At Brighton once she was approached by a man who told her he worked with the Lalique glass people in Paris. He wanted to sculpt her in the nude, holding an orb above her head.

She agreed, and sat, or rather stood for him a few times. Later she discovered that the finished work depicted her in a swimsuit (with stripes) and the symbolic orb had become a beach ball of coloured glass with a bulb inside. It was not Lalique.

'Damn cheek,' she said ruefully. 'He's turned me into a bloody lampstand.' It was a best-selling line.

We packed and moved out, leaving no forwarding address. I thought of Shorty coming back to what he already called 'home'; turning the key, calling out. He would stop, puzzled and then distraught, at the sight of the empty rooms, the open wardrobe, the abandoned nest.

115

I saw him stoop to pick up some forgotten article, a scarf of Mo's, a stocking. Lift it to his face and breathe in the odour as I had seen him do sometimes. Begin to cry, in that irritating, sniffling way.

All for the best, of course. Probably he went home and married a nice girl. Or perhaps he was blown up or gunned down in Burma and would have had no future anyway. Whatever the next step though, it is that moment I think about, that sinking, sickening moment of realization that we had betrayed him.

I see that I am emerging as something of a prig. This is accurate. I was. But I was not a prig all the time: on some days I argued back childishly, stubbornly, or whined. Or remained silent when words were expected – 'dumb insolence', she called it. Sometimes I was perverse – or rather, I *assume* I was, for sometimes she hit me, and even Mo would not have hit me for mere good behaviour.

Her method was unvarying: first, the outraged dignity: 'How dare you speak to me like that/lower your voice/go to your room' (if I had one at the time).

Then the warning: 'You're not too big to be spanked.'

She grabs the child, pushes her, face down, across her knees and pulls down her knickers. Sometimes this is done in the presence of the current man. Always it is when her mother is full of gin. ('O Thou who didst with Pitfall and with gin/Beset the Road I was to wander in' – amazing how apt Fitzgerald's Khayyám could be!)

She begins to spank the child's bottom: hard, stinging blows. The child struggles, kicks, howls, tears falling. The punishment is two-fold: the pain of the beating itself, and the humiliation of the exposed buttocks; the

116

re-statement of who holds the reins. Then, freeing the child, 'Say you're sorry!'

Crying, hiccupping, 'I'm sorry.'

I was not sorry. I was never sorry. I was simply biding my time, to leave, to be free of her. Counting the years, the months, the days. And memory does not play me false. By this time I was counting.

We possessed no radio; never saw the newspapers. The War was something hazy that went on in Europe, involving Hitler and Mr Churchill. In the bazaar where I picked up my news it was Gandhi they were concerned with. Gandhi arrested, Gandhi imprisoned. Even Pearl Harbour and Singapore seemed to have little to do with us.

Riots took place more frequently now and sometimes I was caught in them. Usually the rioters passed – high-pitched screaming, eyes and faces wild, wooden *lathis* cracking against each other and the heads of the unsympathetic.

Calcutta was Kalighat at the beginning, named after the steps of Kali, where the worshippers of the goddess descended from the bank to the waters of the Ganges. The goddess of death and destruction is depicted black, smeared with blood. She has red eyes, four arms, matted hair, fang-like teeth and a protruding tongue that drips with blood. She wears a necklace of skulls; ear-rings of corpses and a girdle of snakes. A fitting goddess for men possessed by the madness of rioting. Squeezed into a doorway I watched them seething like some tangled mass of worms and beetles, battling, squirming, rending. Once they flayed a man after chasing him to the rooftop next to ours. They burned and smashed. It was not at all like Mr Gandhi's passive resistance and civil disobedience.

But it was part of the same message: time to leave.

*　　*　　*

117

December 1942. New flat. New leaf. Christmas to be celebrated in style. Normally Moti cared more about Hogmanay – the Scots rated New Year higher than a mere birthday celebration, it seemed. But this one was to be special, for me. Money had been set aside, tucked into the inner pocket of her handbag. For a few days she had decided to play the role of Mother.

On the night of 20 December the Japanese bombed Calcutta. It should hardly have come as a surprise, much less seemed unthinkable, but no one had thought to prepare, to warn, advise.

The Kidderpore docks, where Indians in their hundreds slept, sheet-shrouded on the pavements and in the open-sided huts, received direct hits. In London, the *Luftwaffe* came in waves; the city was pounded by an armada of flying death machines.

The Japanese used just nine bombers; they flew in, dropped their load and departed. Barges blazed on the Hooghly. We heard the noise of the explosions, the crash and rumble, although faintly. Someone thought it might be an earthquake.

Casualties, we learned later, were 'light' and in comparison with the Bengal famine of the year before, deaths were negligible. But while Indians could be stoical in the face of death that came slowly, silently, that grew out of fever or pestilence or drought, they had no experience of sudden death screaming from a black sky – shrapnel, flames, explosions. These were unknown terrors, unacceptable.

As the docks burned and buildings crashed to the ground, people fled the city, panic stricken. Thousands streamed out of Calcutta, bundles on heads, belongings piled on carts where available. Everything came to a halt. On the deserted streets, in abandoned offices, the whole fragile network of normal life was ruptured. Smoke hung over the silent docks, the streets were littered with refuse left to rot, uncollected, attracting rats, spreading infection. Now, it seemed, the war was real.

There were four more attacks. Some did greater damage but that first one broke the spirit of the street dwellers. It did something else: it brought home what Mr Jinnah and the Muslim League as well as Gandhi's Congress had been pointing out for some time; it was the British who were drawing the Japanese fire. If the British left, the Japanese would leave India alone.

For the first time I felt like a foreigner.

It is Christmas Eve. Shops are open again, life goes on. Moti leaves early to do the Christmas shopping. She has a list: turkey, iced cake, a good sized tree and baubles to decorate it made from spun glass, silver wire and silk. Presents for everyone, some to be kept secret till the morning.

She is gone a long time. The afternoon passes and at dusk Maggie begins to keep watch at the window. She feeds the baby and changes his nappy; with nowhere to hang wet clothes she sometimes finds a used nappy has dried out and pins it on him a second time. When fresh urine wets the yellowish area of old, dried urine, a pungent smell of ammonia fills the air.

Shortly before ten a rickshaw pulls up outside the flat; the rickshaw wallah – unusual, this – helps the passenger out. In the lamplight Maggie sees it is Moti. She is covered in mud, her face and hair caked with dried blood. Her knees are cut and grazed, dried blood streaks her legs. She has lost a shoe. She has no handbag tucked beneath her arm and she carries no presents or shopping bags.

The day had begun well. She got the turkey and bought fresh and crystallized fruit, a cake armoured in glistening royal icing, piped with snowy slopes on which miniature sledges carried scarlet gnomes. She bought an enormous doll in a box; a bird in a cage that sang

119

when you wound up the handle; bright wooden beads to hang on the cradle and a mass of things to put in a stocking. She had three huge shopping bags full, and her last purchases were a tall tree and an armful of glittering balls in a nest of tissue.

Triumphant, she realized that it was still early – mid-afternoon – and she deserved a reward. She would pop into Firpo's for a drink before going home. Leaving the shopping with a porter she sank gratefully into a soft armchair and downed her gin. There were, inevitably, people she knew, and one drink led to another.

But she was not drunk when she sailed out of Firpo's and gave orders for her purchases to be stowed in a taxi. Not drunk, exactly, merely a little hazy and in no mood to object to a second man in the front seat. She climbed into the cab and gave the driver the address.

She may have dozed but she jolted awake, startled, as the car began to bounce over rutted ground at some speed. It was almost dusk, but she could see that they were driving over a patch of wasteland on the far side of the Maidan – nowhere near the flat.

Somehow, without slackening speed, they managed to open the rear door and fling her out of the taxi head first. Only when they realized that she had held on to her handbag, firmly wedged in her armpit as usual, did they stop the cab, leap out and come after her. She should not, of course, have resisted. That was when they attacked her.

Moments later, they drove off, leaving her face down in the mud, weeping, bleeding, half-blinded by the blood trickling from the gash in her scalp.

The doctor is severe: people should know better. Two men in one taxi . . . it was against the law, and at the moment, with anti-British feelings running high . . . Well, no real harm done, luckily. A nasty crack on the head and she ought to stay in bed for a few days.

She lies very quiet, sedated but not asleep. Maggie makes her a cup of tea and holds it while she sips. Her mother's lids are lowered, she seems to be studying the surface of the tea, the tea-leaves bobbing and circling on the surface.

Maggie says apologetically, 'I should have used the strainer –'

Without force or emotion Moti says, her voice tired, 'I'm sorry, monkey. I really meant it to be a special Christmas this time.' Tears trickle, falling onto the sheet, into the teacup.

Next morning, early, the child goes out, leaving mother and baby asleep. She carries a powder puff box which contains a number of tightly folded rupee notes. This is most certainly a 'contingency'. A pity about the accident; nevertheless she is determined to have Christmas as planned, a proper Christmas, the sort she has read about.

She haggles in the bazaar for an undersized chicken, a cake with pinkish streaky icing, a teddy bear no bigger than a pineapple made of bright yellow synthetic fur. She makes sure she gets a present for herself: a black tin paintbox and brush – 'Made in England,' the stallholder says proudly, 'see.' She gets a tiny phial of powerful rose scent and a Christmas tree of sorts, about fifteen inches high. This last, in fact, she gets for nothing, thrown in with the scent.

Home, the two of them open the packages together, on her mother's bed, Moti exclaiming in wonder at it all and even rather gingerly dabbing a – very small – spot of attar of roses behind each ear.

She finds a couple of necklaces and a string of pearls to decorate the tree and gets out of bed, wobbly on her feet, to deal with the chicken. There are no potatoes, but there is, on the other hand, a cake.

There is no gin and none can be bought: the powder puff box is empty.

They feed the baby, eat the chicken straight from the roasting tin, and they cut the cake. Moti is clear eyed, jolly, full of good intentions: what fun this is, she discovers happily, why don't they do it more often? She lies back on plumped-up pillows while Maggie laboriously combs her hair, avoiding the jagged, bloody scab painted purple by the doctor. Moti sings nursery rhymes, summoning up her lost Scots accent for some of them:

> 'One day as I sat in my umba-jumba chamber,
> I saw a raticum-paticum eating my haticum-paticum
>   paynee.
> If I hadna' my stick, ma stole, ma stick, ma stole, ma
>   staynee,
> I'd have beaten that raticum-paticum,
> For eating my haticum-paticum paynee . . .'

It is, indeed, a very special Christmas.

Connections. If it had not been for Shorty's Holy Bible I would not have been in St Paul's singing hymns that Sunday. If it had not been for Shorty losing his head over Moti, the captain would not have come calling to warn her off.

And in that case he would not have recognized me after Sunday service, as we slowly filed out into the sunlight.

'Aren't you . . . haven't we met?'

Tapping his swagger-stick, trim in his peaked cap, the captain smiled, friendly, avuncular.

Maggie stares up at him. She dislikes him because he has separated them from Shorty, so she says nothing. He persists, glancing left and right.

'Do you come to services on your own?'

'Yes.'

'Why?'

'Because I like the singing.'

He sighs. 'I mean, where is your mother?'

'With the baby.'

A look of concern, remorse perhaps, passes over his face. 'I didn't know there was a baby.' He walks with her a few yards. 'I suppose you've found another flat?' Pause. 'I tell you what, I'll see you home.'

If I had wanted to protect him, if I had cared about his peace of mind, his career, his happiness, I could have ducked into the crowd, lost him in a second. He would have wondered, searched a little, shrugged, gone on his way. But I minded about Shorty; I had never thanked him for the bible, had had no chance to say goodbye, kiss the scarred cheek.

He would probably have cried – he cried so easily. I minded, about Shorty. So I nodded, and led the way home.

They have moved to the city's most elegant quarter, to a house that belonged to a diplomat before the new alignments of war took him hurriedly away.

The dining table is black glass, painted with garlands of pink roses. The slender black chairs are lacquered with pink floral decoration and mother-of-pearl inlay. There are wall panels with tigers peering through long grass; dull gold leaf lights up a screen of Japanese silk. It is all a bit much, but there are servants, someone to do the laundry, a cookhouse in the compound and the kitehawks swoop on food as it is carried across to the house, attempting to snatch it off the serving dish. It is just like Amaryllis except that the captain takes Moti dancing. He is rather young and does not drink – yet. On Sundays he takes Maggie to church, before they have lunch.

123

'How old are you, Maggie?'

'She's n—'

'Ten. I was ten last birthday.'

Moti looks murderous but stops short of actually contradicting the child. The captain nods.

'Where do you go to school? You don't seem to have gone, lately.'

Ringing silence. Moment of truth. She avoids looking at Moti. Her chest feels tight. 'I don't go to school.'

He glances at Moti, baffled. 'But when did you last . . .?'

And here it is, without effort. Without magic. The captain, whom she has learned to call Patrick, has waved a swagger-stick wand and she is to go to school, to Miss Juniper Banks' school for British Boys and Girls. It has not been easy: the war has changed much, including passages home to school, and Miss Banks has full classrooms.

No uniform, alas, and no tall Victorian building with gables, playing fields and gym. Miss Banks' establishment was housed in her airy bungalow and the numbers were modest, but it was school!

Patrick took me along to meet her and I fell in love immediately with Miss Banks, with her pale reddish-gold hair, her light green eyes and fair skin dusted with golden freckles. She looked like Greer Garson in *Blossoms in the Dust* and smelled of flowers, and her eyes sparkled with pleasure when I read aloud from a book she handed me.

'Oh, very good! She's very advanced.' Turning to me, 'Do you read a lot, Margaret?'

'Yes.'

'What have you read?'

'*Alice*, and *What Katy Did*, and *Gulliver's Travels* –'

'Good! Yes?'

124

'Um . . . *The Rubáiyát* of Omar Khayyám –'

'*Really!* Goodness me.' Slight consternation. 'Anything else?'

'*The De—*'

Some instinct made me pause: something told me *The Decameron* might not make Miss Banks clap her hands with pleasure.

'Yes?'

'Er, D-Daniel Defoe . . . *Robinson Crusoe.*'

Well, I had *almost* read it; I had seen it in the club library, and I would be sure to read it, now.

'Splendid.' Encouraged, I threw in Buchan, Dumas, Brontë. All splendid.

And then at last, the classroom.

She has an exercise book and a maths text book. 'Page twenty-five. Do the first five exercises.'

Around her books are opened, pencils taken up, fingers and hands move busily. Maggie stares at page twenty-five. She looks at figures set out in pretty patterns. As well as numbers there are letters . . . (a) and (b) . . . x and y . . . She has no idea what is required of her. It might as well be Sanskrit.

After a while the teacher notices. 'Margaret, do you need some help?'

'I'm not *quite* sure how –'

'Just try, don't worry if you can't do them all.'

She picks up the pencil and copies out the patterns of numbers. She does this carefully but she is unaccustomed to it and her efforts look untidy, wobbly. She decides to draw faces in the margin to cheer up the page. The lesson ends at last.

'You mean you don't know how to do equations at all?'

'. . .'

'Multiplication?'

' . . . '

'Division? Subtraction? You can *add up*?'

They are angry; they seem to think it is her fault, that she has deceived them somehow. Her reading was so good, they thought . . . well, nothing else to do now but try and teach her a few basic sums, she must try and catch up. She is given a large illustrated book in which some horrible old elephant in a baggy suit does things to help children add up and take away.

The others laugh at her, a girl of ten with a Babar sum book. The teacher ignores her. Finally they move her down: she sits, looming, a giant among six-year-olds, laboriously learning how figures work, their mysterious properties, the way they cunningly transform themselves and grow larger and smaller – Alice all over again.

In break time we wandered about Juniper Banks' very English garden, ate biscuits, drank fresh lime juice and gossiped. I listened closely, copying the way they spoke, learning the code of talking like a child.

Miss Banks employed two *malis* who worked non-stop to keep the lawn brilliant, the flower beds moist. Here there were no orange cannas with their exotic, dark-red leaves, no bougainvillaea. Miss Banks persevered with a herbaceous border, she took pride in her roses. At break time she sometimes strolled in the garden, bending to sniff a bloom, dead-head or pull out a weed.

Some of the children were discussing Miss Banks' shape: she had swelled alarmingly beneath her flowery smock. They seemed remarkably ill informed.

'She's pregnant,' I said helpfully.

A pause. They cluster, asking questions. Maggie is surprised that children who know about quadratic

126

equations seem ignorant of such simple things as where babies come from and how they are made.

'She has a hole between her legs,' she explains. 'We all have – well, girls do. When the baby's big enough, it pushes out of the hole – the one the blood sometimes comes out of, you know.'

Silence. They stare, listen, astonished. Blood? Some begin to giggle. But how does the baby . . .?

'Oh, some man pushes his –'

Uproar. Scandal. Miss Banks sits at her mahogany bureau and looks at Maggie; serious. Sad.

'I'm disappointed, Margaret. We had high hopes of you. Even with the maths problem . . . But I'm afraid . . . We have had complaints from parents, some of the children have been very upset . . . I didn't expect you to be silly; having a baby is not something to make fun of.'

Her green eyes are not sparkling today and she looks pasty, upset. Maggie is stunned. She tries to explain: it never occurred to her that it was *funny*. She has seen too many women in the bazaar, sick with pregnancy, babies starving or dying –

Hurriedly, Miss Banks breaks in: 'Perhaps it would be better if your parents took you away, found somewhere else –'

'No! *Please*. I don't want to leave. Please let me stay.' The child's face is strained and fierce, her voice thick. *Please*.

Miss Banks considers. She twiddles a paper-knife, shifts correspondence a fraction of an inch.

'Very well. I'll give you another chance. On one condition: I cannot risk the other children being . . . upset by anything you might tell them. So you must give me your word of honour that you will not speak to them during break.'

*

I knew about word of honour. Moti – who never kept a promise she could break; who could be relied on only to let you down – Moti had taught me about word of honour. Once given, you kept it. Moti, who could not tell fact from fantasy in her life, had taught me about lying too: you didn't tell lies. You just didn't.

So now, when I gave pretty, disappointed Miss Banks my word of honour, she may have had doubts about my keeping it, but I had none.

Here was the ultimate irony: I was at school where I had longed to be, surrounded by my peers, by freely chattering boys and girls – and I was forbidden to talk to them. A new sort of glass bell.

But.

Save your sympathy; school was a world I drank in greedily each day. School and all that went with it: I left the house before Moti was up. Rickshaw to the club (ah, respectability! We belonged to the Saturday Club), a plunge into the pool, water closing over my head . . .

Hindus believed the Ganges healed and cleansed them of their sins. This was my Ganges, chlorinated, sparkling.

I rose, cleansed, purified; swam up and down slowly for a while, munched hot buttered toast by the poolside, water streaming off my body through the wicker easy chair into a puddle beneath me.

Then a walk to school, hair dripping wet. At my desk, as I opened my book, trickles of water ran down my neck, zigzagged down my back, soaking my dress, calming, cool.

Now then: the first five exercises . . .

After school there was the cinema. I had pocket money to spare now and Hollywood was right there, in bright, clean, air-conditioned pleasure domes, neon lit and glittering. On the pavement were beggars, blind hollow eyes, empty stomachs, leprosy, flies, pie-dogs, cries of distress, the punishment of heat. Inside . . .

When I went back, later, everything had changed. Where was the Roxy? The Metro? The Trocadero? Have I even got the names right?

Glowing picture palaces with lobbies as big as a compound, thickly carpeted, opulently papered, with soaring roofs and pompous indoor columns, where I spent my afternoons with Rita Hayworth, Joan Crawford, Bette Davis – *The Girl with Red Hair, Now Voyager* – with July Garland and Micky Rooney, Tarzan!

The seats were velvet soft; the miracle of air-conditioning created zephyrs of cool silk. The lighting had a gauzy orange luminosity, like a lurid sunset on a hazy day. The curtains glided smoothly apart, the screen was . . . not silver, but magical. Capable of revealing wonders, obliterating the here and now. Technicolor made real life look dim.

There were other cinemas too, where the audience sat on benches, noisy, fanning themselves to keep cool, where the heat and light of the day penetrated frequently through doors that banged open and shut to admit late-comers. The films at Indian cinemas were quite different: black and white and full of music and dancing, even at the unlikeliest moments.

And whereas even the icing-sugar and glycerine figures of Jeannette Macdonald and Nelson Eddy were allowed to fade out happily ever after with a lingering embrace, no one in Indian movies ever kissed. They played peek-a-boo round conveniently forked tree-trunks, they smiled or scowled, widened their eyes and waggled their heads in a frenzy of emotion, but lip did not touch lip when lovers met or parted. This seemed surprising, but less surprising than the moment when I gazed up at the newest young dancing hero, clad in

129

glistening white, and recognized Saiid, the houseboy from Amaryllis, the one who told the ayah he wanted to be a dancer. He who fled, catching the Royal Doulton plate Moti flung at his head.

'Margaret-Rose wants to be a ballet-dancer. I talked to Alicia Markova about it and she –'

Moti may or may not have talked to Alicia Markova: certainly I was no nearer the Ballet Russes than I had been at four. But Saiid was a star. A little plumper – Indians wanted there to be no ambiguity about the well-fed affluence of their idols – he spun and stamped and smouldered. Happy. And we cheered and clapped, a happy audience.

In Park Street there were two cemeteries, one British, one French. I spent hours in the British cemetery, reading the inscriptions on ornate Victorian tombstones, studying the grandiose monuments, just wandering the overgrown paths between the graves. It was all rubbed and softened by time. Grime, decrepitude and trailing creepers romanticized these confident farewell gestures and gave them a pathos they would have lacked when new and clean. It bothered Moti that I spent so much time in the cemetery but Patrick – part Irish – seemed to understand the appeal.

In any case, the valedictory mood was appropriate, for – though I did not know it then – time was running out for us. We were going home.

Going home. I could no longer imagine what we would find there: the old memories – the opera for Moti, the park, the hotel – had been overlaid by headlines, by rumour: blitzkrieg . . . rationing . . . blackout . . . evacuees, these were all foreign words, I could find no explanations for them, what they would mean to us.

London was in ruins, some people said; there would be whalemeat steak, people sleeping on Underground platforms like Indians here . . .

The German war had seemed a long way off, but now we were to face it, one way and another. For example, U-boats.

We would go home in a convoy, Patrick told us, we would be quite safe, but one could not rule out the possibility – just the possibility – that we might encounter U-boats. This was his way of saying that we might be sunk.

But before we went to meet the war, it came closer, quite suddenly: Japanese warships in the Bay of Bengal, another raid, and Patrick on a quite routine administrative mission, wounded.

'Repatriation,' Patrick said. 'It's an ill wind . . .'

But was it? Would we *like* being home?

'Home,' Moti said, looking thoughtful, excited. 'We'll get there in winter.'

She found a big blue blanket in the bazaar – cheap, felt-like stuff that would have served well to keep a horse warm – and took us round to the *dirzi* to get coats made up, one for me, and a tiny one for the baby.

They stand sweating in the sun, the baby unsteady on his feet – he can balance but not walk yet – and Maggie, holding his hand while the *dirzi* pins and fits the bulky blanket-wool coat on her. The sweat trickles down her neck; people pause to stare curiously. A few yards away, a man having a tooth pulled out, seated in the open-air dental chair, is left waiting, mouth wide, while the dentist investigates these curious costumes. Coats. To below the knee. Buttoning to the neck. Well, well.

131

Above the bright blue wool coat the baby's eyes are like two scraps of the cloth, his ginger hair shines. The material is cheap but warm; it will serve.

It will have to. Patrick has discovered the realities of life with Moti. He occasionally finds himself 'a bit strapped for cash, just for the moment. If they say anything at school, the fees will be along in a few days . . .'

Parties are expensive, and he and Mo do go in for parties. Parties and good times. And bad times. The quarrels, the furious demands – 'Apologize!' The forehand-backhand.

But there were also reconciliations, the unsteady embraces, the heaving and the gasping, the – what did Boccaccio call it? – finding solace in each other, the crying out and the deep, stertorous breathing that followed.

And then, unexpectedly, a wedding dress was to be made. Patrick, an Irish patriarch beneath the youthful, clean-shaven jauntiness, was determined to make an honest woman of her. More to the point, it was the only way to get us back to England.

'Do you mind?' she asked me.

'Would it make any difference if I did?'

She looked shocked. 'Of course! I wouldn't go through with it if you didn't –'

'I like him.'

'He's very fond of you. He knows I care more about you than anything else.'

How tired I had grown of that fantasy. She reacted to my sceptical look.

'You must know that.'

How should I? What sign, what proof, what evidence was there? And perversely, I wanted her to mention the baby. He, too, was important, was he not?

132

'Oh, of course. But you . . . you were the one I wanted.'

So, a wedding dress of stiff tussore, short to the knee as was the fashion, with puffed shoulders and a hat tipped over her nose. Sling-backed, peep-toed, platform-soled shoes. In the wedding photograph, eyes screwed up against the glare, she looks grotesque, but happy.

Another snapshot: a mother and child, a baby whose ginger curls are bleached white in the sunlight. It is an exterior, a beach, and in the background, bending to the sand, a skinny, straggly-haired girl, thin, long arm extended, is frozen in the act of picking up a shell. She is intent, and her left hand, cupped, holds a cluster of gleaming mother-of-pearl.

All that holiday I collected shells. 'The seaside,' Patrick said; 'we shall all have a holiday at the seaside before going home.'

It seemed an eccentric idea, to spend days and nights in the train in order to sit in the sun. People kept out of the sun here, this was not Dorset or Brighton. But it worked. There were mysteries to that beach: the miles of empty sand and strange creatures – bulging jellyfish and fish that blew themselves up like balls, and living bags of prickles – and, growing from the dunes, cliffs hollowed out to make fantastic carvings: caves, temples, statues, gigantic faces staring blindly out to sea, all carved from solid rock. It faced east and at sunrise the first light fell on the carvings, staining them vermilion.

We stayed at a monastery, shaded by a grove of palm trees, and there was nothing to see but the empty beach, the sea and the crumbling, mysterious carvings.

The wind blew constantly, gritty, stinging, and we dug pits in the sand, one for the baby to lie in, sheltered from the wind. One day a sudden gust stronger than usual sprayed him thickly with sand so that he looked like an effigy newly revealed by an archeologist's hand, or like a Pompeian child, found in a shallow grave, sealed in an attitude of slumber. Then he yawned, and a wet, pink hole opened in the sandy skin like a wound.

There was another pit for grilling giant prawns over charcoal, but the wind seasoned them with sand and our teeth screeched and grated as we chewed them.

Hour after hour the breakers rolled onto the empty sand, crashing, pausing, withdrawing, then a slow gathering, and the next foaming, thunderous breaker bowed onto the sand, the surf like the waving plumes on a musketeer's hat.

I collected shells, keeping them in a strong paper bag. There were hundreds, each different: some long and attenuated, like a treble clef; others conical, brilliant with colour – pearl, pink, blue, violet. They lay in a shining heap, the smallest a fragile saucer smaller than the nail on my little finger, the largest a conch as big as my fist, speckled brown and white with smooth blunt teeth like a dog's mouth. Holding it to my ear I heard another ocean growl softly, blotting out the breakers and the surf.

For a few days Moti enjoyed the beach. She lay, exhausted; she bathed, knowing sea-water was good for her arthritis. We played games, throwing quoits, a ball. Once, out of breath, she paused, balancing the beach-ball above her head: she was thicker in the body, but her legs had kept their shape. For a moment I saw her as she had been in Dorset, the breeze blowing the tawny hair across the laughing mouth, grey-green eyes shining like wet pebbles.

It was as though she read my thoughts because she stretched up, pulling in her sagging stomach muscles, and called over to Patrick, 'I posed nude for a man once, like this . . . he said I would be immortalized in Lalique glass.' She laughed and threw him the ball. 'Turned out

134

to be a bloody barbola lampstand, with a bulb stuck in the beach ball!'

Perhaps the memory proves unsettling, for that night Moti and Patrick somehow organize a taxi to take them to the nearest town, and when it drops them back, late, at the monastery, Moti carries a bag that chinks glassily.

Next day there is unpleasantness: the monks are upset, the guests are asked to leave. There is time for a last trip to the beach, a few more treasures to be scooped up, brittle, glittering, nacreous; oblongs and triangles, filigreed pipes, immaculate spirals and whorls.

Clutching her now heavy brown paper bag the child climbs into the taxi that will take them to the station. The sun's fierce beam from directly overhead has put out the eyes of the idols carved from the cliffs; their black, empty sockets stare blindly out to sea.

In the train, with its big zinc tub of ice on the compartment floor, she once again examines the shells: among them is a pearly nautilus, and Patrick explains how the spiral is formed by the occupant, building out from a single chamber, adding a new cell each time the previous one is outgrown.

'It's attached so tenuously to its shell,' he says, holding the empty silvery whorl on the palm of his hand, 'that it's pretty vulnerable . . . easily detached.'

Maggie squats next to the zinc tub, washing the shells, rinsing them in the melted ice water, rubbing them dry one at a time. There is no need to hurry.

The baby had a name, Nicholas, but no one used it, perhaps because Moti had never got round to having him baptized. To me, he was just 'baby', my substitute for all the dolls and toys left behind with the luggage in moonlight flits, or retained by cautious hotels 'pending settlement of the account'. He was my creature. I gave

135

him his bottle, changed his nappy and sang him to sleep, hour after hour.

It sometimes took so long that I wonder now whether in fact I might have been keeping him awake with the singing; whether he might have dropped off sooner without it.

Curled up on the floor next to the cot I would run through the repertoire I had learned from Moti.

> 'Button up your overcoat when you're on the spree;
> Take good care of yourself, you belong to me . . .'

There were songs she no longer sang: 'Down in the Canebrake', 'Go to Sleep, My Baby' (a Paul Robeson hit), 'Shortnin' Bread'. Curious to realize now that all this was black American music, passed on to me by someone who professed to despise things American and mistrusted blacks.

On very wakeful nights, when the little blue boot-button eyes stayed fixed on mine I gave him the full ten verses of 'Wraggle-Taggle Gypsies' and followed through with my own vocal version of the Gold and Silver Waltz by Franz Lehar. I learned the tune from a recording by Andre Kostelanitz which Patrick brought home one day and played until the record got chipped. But with my sharp ear I had already mastered it note for note.

'La la . . . la la la . . . la la la . . . la la la . . .'

On the other side was the overture to *Cavalleria Rusticana*, but even I could not achieve much of an approximation to that.

He was in general well behaved: like me, he knew instinctively that Moti would not look kindly on tears or whining. When we travelled together he sat on my lap or on the seat, propped up between us. The small blue eyes looked about eagerly, at first from face to face, and then, after a while, taking in the wider world beyond the window. I looked forward to talking to him – in fact I talked to him already, but he had not yet managed to keep up his end of the conversation. I planned to begin his education early. 'Mathematics is *most* important. We shall start with the multiplication tables and then . . .' It was all a bit like Alice talking to Dinah the cat.

The monsoon was expected. There was a breathlessness, a stillness in the air. A sudden wind would whip up dead leaves, dust. People were edgy. Copper-coloured clouds piled up, angry, curdled looking. The winds waited with full lungs; the gods were ready. Somewhere, a signal, like the releasing downward beat of the bandleader, and the rains came down.

Solid sheets of water hammered, drumming on the roof, blotting out landscape and sky, turning the world to liquid. The rain crashed down and from the inundated earth came an overpowering smell of wetness.

We took a gharry into the centre of town; Moti nervy as she so often was at monsoon time, the baby and I. The rain thrummed on the taut roof of the gharry and the horses strained against the pull of the flood, stumbling.

Beneath our wheels the road was over a foot deep in water; water that scoured out new pot-holes in the already poor surface. The wheels tilted, jolting the carriage violently. At one of these jolts, quite slowly but too fast for a restraining hand to prevent it, the baby slid off the seat between us. I grabbed at his romper suit but the material was stretched too tight over his nappy to give my fingers a purchase.

He bounced off the floor of the gharry and vanished beneath the swirling yellow-brown water. We screamed to the driver, dived after him from the still-moving carriage, clawing and groping, fingers scraped raw on protruding stones, and then I saw a muddy tangle of curls, grabbed, hauled, and pulled him up like a sodden bundle of old clothes, coughing, choking, covered with thick brown mud that clogged his eyes, nose, mouth.

He looked like an earthenware statue, some child deity dug up out of the river's slime. His mouth, mud filled, was open but he was not crying. On the beach he had turned suddenly to a sandstone figurine; dragged from the flood he seemed made of mud and water. On each occasion, for a moment, I felt a sudden sharp pain. My heart seemed to twist. And then he moved; I saw him breathe and breathed again.

He had swallowed a lot of water and the hospital wanted to keep him in overnight. Moti slept in the room with him.

Next day he looked better but his temperature remained high and I heard a curious sound when he breathed. He blazed with heat, there was congestion, they said. Opinions were expressed, decisions taken, the small bundle was moved from one room to another. Then, undramatically, he was dead.

I would not, after all, teach him multiplication tables; hear secrets, find out what he was thinking all those months while he waited for the gift of speech. It was the worst of moonlight flits and he was the one who had gone, leaving us behind, holding his things.

We knew each other. I was waiting to show him wonders, explain, teach, share. I felt, as I had felt that day in the gharry, the last of him slip through my fingers.

The last weeks are oddly blurred: no details remain, I can recall no last walk round the bazaar or Park Street cemetery, no farewell speech from Miss Banks, who had warmed to me in the end. There were riots, disturbances, demonstrations: British Go Home. Yanks too. Mr Gandhi advises . . . Mr Nehru . . . Mr Jinnah . . . but I remember only shadows, a sense of blanking out.

Packing there must have been, though not all that much: my beautiful dolls languished in custody in various far-away hill station guest houses and hotels, as did the smooth wooden building bricks; the black tin paintbox was used up. I borrowed books from the club library.

My only precious possessions were Shorty's bible, the ivory lace dress, carried safely from one end of the country to the other, unworn but undamaged by moth or monsoon damp. And my collection of shells.

They sat in the crumpled paper bag, crunching when moved, the sound like shingle underfoot. They were the prize, the magic talisman I would carry back to that mysterious country which once again, it seemed, was to be 'home'.

'I think you should go and stay with your father for a bit. Say goodbye,' Moti said brightly.

'?'

Why? And did he even want to see me? It seemed so. Grown-ups, communicating mysteriously, had come to an agreement about their wishes, had arranged it.

These days, parents, democratic, liberal, educated to awareness of children-as-people, do not lightly parcel them up, ship them off, dispose without consultation. I consider my children's wishes, their needs. My own experience was sharply different.

'O'Grady says do this' – and I did it.

'O'Grady says go there' – and I went.

(Much later I wondered whether – that time – I had been unfair to them: whether getting me away was kindly meant, a change of scene to take my mind off things.)

Travelling with a military wife I took the train, the seats hot and sticky, scratching the backs of my knees and bare legs. In the night, sleeping as the train rocked its way over a steeply curved bridge, I was thrown off the bunk into the big zinc tub full of half-melted ice. Shocked awake, water in my mouth, I thought I was drowning. I saw yellow-brown water, a tangle of mud-soaked curls. I choked and screamed, startling the military wife.

At dawn the pink sun swelled like a slow balloon above the dust-grey horizon. Lucknow station came into view, and I was handed over.

He looked older. Of course he *was* older, but . . . the leathery cheeks were more deeply lined and creased, the heavy shoulders more bowed than I remembered. He still had that ambiguous, secret grin, suddenly lifting all the lines in his face upwards; the shining brown eyes my grandfather had suspected so inaccurately of being lascivious still had a deceptive glint.

We stood awkwardly and finally he kissed my brow, bumping his lip when I raised my head at the wrong moment.

There were words I had rehearsed: should I say them now? Can I stay with you? Would you have me? Too sudden; better to leave it a while.

'Well!' he said.

The word hung in the air, vibrating. How would he follow it up? 'You've grown . . .' or 'You're too thin . . .' If he should ask: 'Are you happy, monkey?' should I say – ?

He glanced at his watch.

'I thought we might eat here, at the station. It's a long drive.'

I discovered I was starving. We ate fried pomfret, crisp and moist, with fried potatoes. Ice cream.

I watched him as I ate. He caught my eye and smiled encouragingly. He looked like a man cudgelling his brains for the right thing to say.

140

'How's the fish?' Fine. Lovely.

'Do you still listen to Beethoven?'

He looked startled. 'Fancy you remembering.'

'Oh, I remember everything.'

'Everything?' He looked doubtful, uneasy almost. To remember everything was surely excessive?

He leaned across the table, 'Do you like music, then? Of course, you're a ballet-dancer, aren't you?'

'I like singing really.'

'Oh! Well you must let me hear something . . .'

'Yes –' No. I wanted to explain: there are plenty of songs, but they all belong to the baby. I can't sing them now, you see.

> *Button up your overcoat when you're on the spree;*
> *Take good care of yourself, you belong to me.*

The chair scraped on the floor as I pushed it hastily away from the table. The lavatory smelled of urine and pine disinfectant. I leaned over the bowl and vomited up the fresh, moist pomfret and the ice cream. Tears ran down my face, hot against my skin, the first I had shed. I must have been in there for quite some time because when I came out, face washed, eyes tight and red, he had ordered coffee and finished it, but he appeared to notice nothing.

'The train must have upset my tummy,' I offered.

'Sorry.'

'We'll go home,' he said.

So we drove home. For here, too, it seemed, was 'home', that looking-glass country.

Lucknow left behind, Cawnpore inching towards us. Amaryllis seemed to have shifted closer to town, there were new bungalows, shops where there had been open ground. The compound looked dusty, small, but a servant at the gate leaped up to salute us as the car swept in. The tree I played beneath was still there, and

141

with a stab of surprise and pleasure I saw that the sandpit was as it had always been, freshly sifted, pristine. I remembered how the sand felt beneath my bare toes, the ayah patiently filling and refilling her brass pot with water so that I could build mud pies. And here it still was. Something of mine, of the past, survived after all.

Up the steps to the veranda, and the cool, chip marble floor of the lounge. And the cool, smiling face of a plain woman in a shapeless print frock. A broad face, like a moon.

'Maggie, this is Jane. You probably remember her as –'

Miss Austell. The dancing teacher. Of course.

'Oh,' I said, thinking of the sandpit, looking at her, everything suddenly clear. 'You're pregnant.'

The smile vanishes. Above her head, the child sees the woman flash her father a look. Oh, Miss Banks. She has done it again.

The look said, loud as words: a savage, a social embarrassment. I heard a door clang shut.

Part Three

The crossing took six weeks. But before that we had more than a month, waiting in Poona. People tell me it is an attractive town with a handsome palace worth a visit. When it was occupied in 1805 by Colonel Arthur Wellesley, better known as the Duke of Wellington, stirring deeds were done, Napoleon's plans were thwarted. But I saw no evidence of its glorious past: I spent four weeks in Poona and never went beyond the wire perimeter of the military transit camp.

Moti roared her way through the entire four weeks: each morning she bowled into town in a horse-drawn tonga and spent the day seeking – and achieving – oblivion. Next day she swam blearily into wakefulness still un-sobered. There was nothing to deflect her. The camp was purgatory: she despised the military wives ('mediocrities and snobs'), she embarrassed the officers, and the men were out of bounds. No parties were possible and even Patrick could devise no distractions that would serve. She did the only thing left to her: she obliterated us all.

We went on board ship around midday. She had reached the mean and quiet stage and only skilled Moti-watchers would have known from the fixed glaze on her eyes, the rolling, stalking gait, that she was about to blow. We negotiated the gangplank carrying the modest amount of luggage permitted in the cabin, and I became aware that Moti's was remarkably heavy and occasion-ally gave out a musical clinking sound.

She had already been given the dreadful news that

there would be no alcohol available on board. The order that none was to be taken on she had decided to ignore.

We reached the cabin, a cramped, four-berth affair and Moti flopped gratefully into the nearest bunk. I studied a card pinned on the door and debated how to break the news.

'I think we're sharing the cabin with two ladies.'

She swivelled her head slowly and focused on me.

'What do you mean?'

'We're sharing –'

'I heard you. But we can't be. That makes five and there are only four berths.'

I looked at the card again. 'I think Patrick must be somewhere else. That's the way they're doing it. We're with the women and children, and –'

'We bloody well aren't.'

She was on her feet, tugging down her dress, wedging her handbag under her arm, and then she was off, weaving and stalking, in search of the Man in Charge.

He was in a small cubicle, harassed, sweating and tired. Several people were waiting to be dealt with but Moti swept straight past them, up to his desk. She began with relative mildness: there must be some mistake . . . hardly sensible . . . splitting up a family . . . quite absurd, really, and so simple to remedy the –

He ruffled his papers and explained tersely that there was no mistake: conditions of war . . . all in the same boat, ha-ha, that while he sympathized, of course, he was sure she would not want special treatment at the expense of others . . . His smile was a punctuation mark. He actually thought the interview was at an end. I watched him pityingly: he had no idea of what was about to happen.

Moti took a deep breath and stood up. She was taller than he was and grew even taller as she spoke, though 'spoke' hardly does justice to her delivery: had she been

144

in a theatre, the last row of the topmost gallery could have relaxed, relishing the audibility of her words. She was Medea, Phèdre, Lady Bracknell. She suggested that the absurd little man before her should listen carefully; she explained that she had no intention of sharing her rat-hole of a cabin with a couple of unknown and possibly halitosis-ridden strangers –

He made to interrupt and her voice grew even firmer.

'I shall have my husband with me, a *not unreasonable* state of affairs!'

Again he tried to break in. This was unwise.

'Be *quiet!*' she thundered. 'If you do not *at once* rearrange the accommodation, I shall simply have to go to your commanding officer – who happens to be a *particular friend of mine* – and tell him you have made a balls-up, not only of *my* accommodation, but of the *entire* embarkation arrangements. I have noticed . . .' She paused and leaned over the desk, blasting him with a lethal dose of Gordon's-loaded breath. 'I have noticed *several* unfortunate mishaps already. No doubt you are aware of what I am referring to, and if the matter comes up you will, I'm *sure*, have a satisfactory explanation . . .'

He blinked rapidly: the bitch was obviously lying, but he was not quite confident enough to call her bluff. She sensed a wavering and drew herself up, towering over him.

'If we do not have our own cabin within the hour, I shall start to get angry.' Pause. 'And make a *noise*.' He flinched. 'If necessary,' she added graciously, 'you can give us a cabin for two. The Child can sleep on the floor.'

It was disgraceful. It was selfish. It was not fair play and it certainly wasn't British. But Moti believed in the justice of her demands, she always did, that was what gave her her strength. The Man in Charge had too many problems already. He decided to avoid one more, and so we became the only family on that crowded troopship to have a cabin to ourselves.

But in one respect it was a pyrrhic victory: the Man in Charge himself arrived to supervise the move, and discovered that curious, heavy clinking in Moti's luggage. The liquor was confiscated, though he did not put it like that. He was polite, even ingratiating.

'I'm sure you were unaware . . . dry ship . . . no alcohol allowed . . . commanding officer, who of course is a friend of yours, most particularly stressed . . .'

She was furious, but she could hardly threaten anything, given that she had smuggled the stuff on board in the first place. His eyes gleamed with satisfaction as the bags were opened and bottle after precious bottle taken away.

For years we had followed the rivers, wandering the subcontinent, meandering like the rivers themselves. The Jumna took us to Deradoon, Allahabad, Delhi and Agra. Sacred in its source and its junctions the Ganges took us to Benares and Calcutta, and at Calcutta there was the Hooghly, sand-banks, and freak tide-wave.

Later, year after year I had a recurring nightmare: a wall of water rushing towards me, hanging over me, a moment of breathless hovering, a sense of imminent inundation, horror. Only much later did I realize that it was inspired by the Hooghly bore, which I had forgotten in my waking hours; the inflowing high-tide rushing against the current like a wall, rising to a height of several feet, surging up-river, swallowing banks, beasts, men.

When I went back, I saw how the river in its various forms was always there in the background: down the road from Amaryllis the Ganges was shallow and muddy. These were the banks where a hundred years earlier British men, women and children were mass-

146

acred, trapped as they struggled through the shallow water towards boats they would never reach. And there we were, still in occupation, though not for long now, in that curious bitter relationship which combined mimesis and rejection; hatred and an illogical loyalty.

At Allahabad, where we had rested for a while, Moti and I, the Ganges was joined by the Jumna on its way from Delhi, and then – broader and more important now – it dawdled past Benares till it found its way to Calcutta. Rivers and railways, these were the magic paths.

The British built the railways; the rivers were always there, shifting and changing and sometimes swelling dangerously to punish us, it seemed, for trying to tame them, contain their power.

The Indians recognized the power; they worshipped and gave thanks, but the rivers punished us all impartially.

Moti's old drinking partner, Ruddy, the Hooghly pilot with the bushy beard, knew the deadly sandbars and the narrow channels in which lay the bones of lost ships and men. 'The ruddy river can't pull any new tricks on *me*,' he said. But one night a bunch of disaffected Swarajists waylaid him and beat him up and threw him in the Hooghly. Conscious, he could have swum to safety. Instead, he floated face down, moving with the movement of the water. In the darkness the blood would have seeped out of his body without staining the water.

Death by drowning. The Hooghly providing a last, fatal embrace.

Later, trying to retrace those early footsteps, I found my way to Connaught Circus. Where Moti's smart bar had been was now a shop catering for tourists, selling package trips to Instant India – all the sights you need to see in six days.

I tried to buy a train ticket to Cawnpore; flirting with the idea of finding my way once more to Amaryllis.

'Cawnpore?' I asked the counter clerk.

He looked baffled, my English delivery of the name misleading him. Then his face cleared. 'Ah, Kanpur,' he said.

I met this all the time: Dehradoon had become Dehra Dun on the maps now; Benares had reverted to Varanasi; Poona was Pune and Karachi was not even in India, but Pakistan. Their country of course, and their right, but dislocating for us exiles, looking for guide-lines to the past. If you change the names, you sever the emotional clue; the forked paths of the labyrinth become too bewildering; we retreat, strangers where once we lived.

'Kanpur?' he repeated. 'Why do you wish to go there? Industrial city, nothing to be seen there.'

I suppose not. And with a sudden loss of nerve I booked instead a ticket on the Taj Express.

'Agra, oh yes. Very good. The Taj Mahal. You will have a nice time.'

On board ship but tied up to the dock we remained for these last few hours still 'in' India. Like a vast corpse the ship moved, rising and falling gently with the water.

Departures are never easy: reluctant, relieved, apprehensive, expectant, whatever the mood, I find them painful affairs. I feel the roots finally wrenching free of the retaining soil; almost I can hear them, a mandrake shriek. Therefore I take steps to protect myself.

So I recall neither the last day at Amaryllis nor the ship pulling away from the dockside, taking us 'home'. Taking us away from what had been home.

There were, no doubt, U-boats and enemy aircraft about, and the convoy took an unusually roundabout route home. There were regular banshee howls from the alarm, which sent us all scurrying to our stations, but as we never

148

knew whether these were genuine alerts or merely prac-
tice runs, we soon became blasé about them.

Moti took to her bunk. She seemed now, suddenly,
to be mourning for the baby. First she had tried to rid
herself of something undesirable; later he had been
treated casually, an appendage, an extra piece of luggage. Now she discovered he had been something more.
This can happen: otherwise engaged, we find too late
we have entertained an angel unawares. And so Moti,
finding out too late, lay with her face to the cabin wall,
sober, and lamented.

I was with her less than usual because the Army,
mindful that Satan finds work, etc., organized lessons
every day in a long, low-ceilinged saloon in the bowels
of the ship. And I had a lot of catching up to do.

One day, mistaking one hatch for another, taking a
wrong turning, I found myself on the troop deck where
the Other Ranks, the soldiers, were billeted: tier upon tier
of bunks, closely packed. No armchairs to relax in; bad
air, fetid from the sweating pores of too many men. No
recreation area, no light. They lay in their bunks or sat,
slumped, skin shiny with sweat, eyes glinting in the dimness, killing time, like galley slaves between shifts. I wondered, as I backed away with an apology, why they were
not up on deck, in the light and the fresh air.

The schoolroom too, was crowded, but more agree-
ably: around us the engines throbbed and turned, the air
filtered noisily through pipes in the ceiling and dozens of
us, all ages, crammed in together, muddled along doing
school work.

I listened, I wrote down, I grappled. I picked up clues,
inching my way through this maze of learning. There
was algebra and – blinding light – geometry and Euclid:
some of the drawings reminded me of the Jantar Mantar
Observatory, and best of all, I understood. QED.

The crossing took six weeks and for one person at

least, was far too short: a period of peace, discovery and adventure.

Between lessons we organized an Entertainment. A concert to be given by the children. I showed them a tap routine for three girls – ('Good morning! Good morning!') demonstrating steps absorbed long ago across the post-breakfast dimness of a hotel dining room as a trio of tired dancers in black satin shorts and fishnet tights pinned on their smiles and rehearsed their tired routine with determined verve. I did magic tricks learned from the gully-gully men in the bazaar; I danced. I sang – not 'Gloomy Sunday', though.

'Very interesting, dear,' said Freddie the producer warmly, 'but . . . the *mood* . . . un peu *triste* . . . not quite . . . How do you feel about "Somewhere Over the Rainbow"?'

Patrick is busy with military matters and Moti is left to herself. As the weather grows cooler she emerges to sit wrapped in a rug spread out on deck. No deck-chairs on board 'in case of enemy action', and no stewards to bring glasses clinking with ice and filled with good cheer. Instead, Moti braces her back against the steel wall and sits quietly, gazing at the horizon. Sometimes Maggie joins her.

Now and then, catching her eye, Moti rouses herself; the long, sad, downward curve of her mouth lifts into a smile, even occasionally into rueful laughter.

And Maggie watches her, aching with apprehension and with dreams. Her mother has managed to get through six weeks: her eyes have lost the sheen that reminds the child of dead fish; they are alive, they reflect her changing mood, and the mood is improving. When they reach England, could this not continue? Become the norm? If certain magic words are invoked, with the most intense concentration . . . or perhaps God should be en-

150

listed here? The services and the music in St Paul's dealt much with Jesus: ask and it shall be given. Seek and ye shall find, etc. She pulls Him into the Grand Plan.

On the day of the concert she unpacks the ivory lace dress and irons it.

Why had she never tried it on? How had she not noticed that it looked smaller somehow than of yore. And, of course, Moti never involved herself in arrangements of this sort.

Maggie slips the lace dress over her head and, with unexpected difficulty, pulls it down . . . and stares aghast in the cabin mirror: hem halfway up her thighs, sleeves revealing inches of wrist and arm. Worst of all: fabric stretched across her chest so tight that fastening the buttons is out of the question. There are the beginnings of breasts, hardly more than a bump and a shallow convexity, but they give her no pride, merely accentuate the disaster.

I cried, I recall with shame, extravagantly. I pulled off the dress and stamped on the fine lace. I picked it up and screwed it into a ball and hurled it against the wall and when I had done that I folded it up again and thrust it down a toilet bowl and nearly caused a flood. It was a disaster to rival the *Titanic*, the *Hindenburg*, a black night of the soul. I searched for violent, colourful words to express my rage, but Moti's vocabulary – in my hearing at any rate – had never been adventurous. 'Bloody hell!' I muttered, kicking the wall. 'Bloody. *Hell.*'

In my mind's eye I saw myself singing the song to end the show: the finale, my triumph. I would be Deanna Durbin, Judy Garland, Kathryn Grayson, all the heroines of the magic screen, radiant in my ivory lace.

Well, I wore my brown cotton with the frilled collar and it did very well. The audience was ready for 'Somewhere Over the Rainbow'; they echoed the words in their minds, and no one believed in them more fervently than the singer. I sang with lungs and heart and soul, the audience joined in the second chorus and when I finished, the applause lasted as long as the song.

I stood there, hearing it beating up at me like a great surf, knowing the waves were crashing and the voices calling just for me, and I turned into liquid fire, a shower of gold, scattering my radiance on them. I had performed before without this metamorphosis, but that had been dancing. To sing, I realized, was to move into a new dimension, breathing air from another planet, cutting free of the dragging problems of reality. Here lay the true magic. In singing.

I suppose I should mention that earlier in the pro-gramme I did a very competent Dying Swan. It was received politely. Moti, thin lipped, slaughtered the audience with a scything glance.

'Bloody philistines,' she said coldly. 'No wonder Nijinsky went mad.'

I stood on the quayside in my bright blue blanket-coat, my breath rivalling the freezing mist shrouding the docks.

England – 'home' – was different this time. Sweet rationing struck me as irrelevant because I had never eaten sweets. But the gaps between houses, the fresh ruins like decayed stumps in a row of teeth, were dis-turbing. People talked of V2s and flying bombs but Moti was brisk about all that and found us a flat in the Earls Court Road. The sounds and sights of war were all around us. And it was nothing like the Calcutta docks.

It was Patrick who insisted we should get out of London and dredged up an old aunt on the Welsh border whose farmhouse was too big for her. Moti and I became PGs; somewhat more genteel than boarding-house inmates, more personal than hotel customers. Paying guests had an uneasy relationship: not quite family, not quite not. The farmhouse was never really warm enough, especially when it snowed, and Moti loathed it, escaping to London and Patrick as often as possible.

She saw no virtue in exercise, what she called 'pointless walks' of the sort I took. We never could talk to each other, so I could not explain to her that I was just discovering the extraordinary tenderness of the English countryside; the weightlessness of leaf-mould flaking, scattering; the moist, dark, crumbling richness of the soil, the difference of texture between the pale, firm primrose petals and the brilliance of the bluebells, so fragile that they almost liquefied beneath the touch of a finger. I did not pick them. I had learned not to, long ago.

'Bloody Jains!' Moti used to exclaim when I held back from killing a spider or a beetle. At Amaryllis there had been the episode of the Jain servant who refused to kill cockroaches and had to go. Later I met other Jains, stood in their temples, saw the nets tied over lamps so that moths would not immolate themselves. Illogically, I went on eating meat. But I could not kill. And I did not pick wild flowers.

I sat among them (crushing grass, but what can one do?) and smelled wet earth, the greenness of things, felt the cool air warming as the earth slowly spun to face the sun.

VE day has come and gone and the war seems to be over. At boarding school Maggie luxuriates in the circumscribed timetable, plays netball and lacrosse, develops a crush on a gaunt sixth-form goddess, the cleverest girl in the school. Ruth is bony and black-haired with a grim, ironical smile that barely lights the black pools of her eyes. She has an exhausted quality which gives her the look of a patient in the terminal phase. As far as Maggie can tell she is not unhappy, or at least she never says so, but she seems wrapped in an invisible garment of mystery and reserve. She broods.

Maggie confides her adoration and anxiety to an older girl who shrugs amiably. 'Oh, you don't want to worry. It's nothing special, they're all like that.'

They?

'She's Jewish. There's always something.'

What was she in mourning for? I wondered. I was an extraordinarily ill-informed child, moving through huge events yet unaware of them. The books I read were set in the past; at home we talked only of trivialities in my hearing. I saw no newsreels. A childish ignorance persisted long after it should have done.

And not till later, too, did I take in that the Japanese, who had come flying in over Kidderpore docks one night, a strike force of nine bombers, who had set fire to fifteen barges and gutted ten dock sheds and set the city in a panic with these modest means, had in due course participated in a larger experiment called Hiroshima.

They had bought a house. While I was at boarding school they had bought a house in Chislehurst (O irony: Moti, so scornful of Michael Arlen's heroine of the pagan body in the Chislehurst mind now found herself, a pagan body *and* mind, in the heart of the place), so now we had a home, a two-storey, nineteen-thirties Tudor with leaded windows and an overgrown garden with lavender bushes and a sagging pergola laden with old-fashioned roses.

I had no inkling that plans had been made: at the end of the summer term Ruth pressed her bloodless lips to mine (we had progressed that far), the grim smile lurked. Clandestine piano lessons were talked of – she could teach me after school hours. We would sit together on the piano stool. There was promise of autumnal magic.

So I said no goodbyes. The news came in passing: I would not be going back. In future I would attend a day school, a small private establishment nearby, cheaper for them and better for me. Better? Indeed. There was an excellent dancing class.

These casual cruelties of domestic life: a kindly man, a woman without wickedness, simply lacking the imagination to put themselves in someone else's place. As with the shells. We have not dealt with the shells.

They are unpacking, strewing over the floor and chairs the possessions carried home across the hostile oceans. And Maggie searches, at first calmly, then anxiously, for the paper bag of shells. At last she says, 'I can't find my shells.'

Moti looks at her absently. 'Shells?'

'The shells from Madras, the shells I collected on the beach. In a brown paper bag.'

'Well, if they're not here you probably left them behind.'

She has a curious sensation in her chest, something hot and burning threatens to burst out of her body.

'But *you* packed everything. I left them with you. *I* was at Amaryllis. You promised to pack them. You *promised*.'

A final broken promise. So many, broken earlier, some of them more important, but this, oddly, the worst. Unimportant in themselves, the discarded armour of dead molluscs, fragments of carbonate of lime and conchin, shards and discs and spirals, the shells were all I had to remind me of a world left behind.

In my fingertips there was a strange prickling; I clenched my fists, holding them to my chest.

Years before, at the little hill station on the shores of the lake, soon after the incident of the Holy Man, a

155

houseboy went berserk one Sunday morning and attacked his elderly British employer with an axe.

Screams, the sound of splintering furniture and shouts bring people running to the house, which can only be approached across a footbridge spanning a deep gully in the hillside.

Across the footbridge the houseboy parades, flourishing an axe, its blade clotted and dark. Behind him, tottering in the doorway is the woman he has attacked, her head wrapped in a towel through which blood is seeping. She whimpers and cries for help, but at the least movement from the people gathering on the other side of the bridge, the houseboy waves the axe in a businesslike way.

'I split her head like an apple!' he shouts.

Maggie watches, fascinated, as the towel darkens with blood, the woman sinks to the ground, eyelids fluttering. For a moment she imagines Moti in the woman's place, skull split open, being held together with a sodden towel. If Moti died, she would be free.

'Like an apple!' the houseboy shouts. Then he begins to cry and he too sinks to his knees.

Once again I felt murder sweep through me: she had promised to pack the shells.

I know I screamed at her, called her names – nothing very terrible; today's children would consider it nursery stuff, today's parents would regard it as grounds for mild remonstrance, but those were the days of feudal authority on the parent front. She lost her temper.

'Lower your voice! And apologize! I will not tolerate – you're not too big to be spanked!'

But I was.

*

156

Voice shaking, eyes hot and moist, the child says, 'If you touch me I will hit you.'

The woman cannot believe her ears. Two strides take her across the room. It is the bathroom and she subsides on the edge of the bath, grabs the child and pushes her, face down, across her knees. But the child's arm has snaked up behind her and the tawny, messy hair is seized and held fast, in fingers twisted to grip the harder.

A silent, fierce struggle: as the woman attempts to pull up the child's dress, pull down knickers. As the child hauls on the hair. Silence, except for the gasping of breath and the sound of individual hairs snapping under that ineluctable tension. To anyone watching, it might look funny: this slow, silent combat, a tableau-vivant – 'The Gladiators' – as the child hangs like a mongoose on the throat of a threshing snake, slowly dragging the woman's head backwards.

Then with a sudden slackening, it ends. The woman hurls the child from her, the child's fingers release the hair, both stagger, avoiding one another's eyes. The episode is never referred to. A corner has been turned.

It was a very English garden we had in Chislehurst, with crazy paving and herbaceous borders, a formal pond where once there had been goldfish, before the cats got them. Over the years it had become neglected, creepers out of control, fruit trees unpruned.

In August, with flowers rioting everywhere, it was filled with colour and drowsy scents, the sound of bird-song. A sleepy, magical place.

When I went back to Amaryllis, for that botched reunion, after the sandpit and the pregnant stepmother had greeted me, I wandered a little. Not too freely: riots were different now; no longer could I watch from a doorway while the street boiled suddenly into violence,

157

as men broke heads and spilled blood in the name of some mysterious, divisive God. Now the riots had another purpose – 'Swaraj' – and it was wiser for outsiders to keep well away.

But there were still places I could go, unnoticed. Here was a high wall remembered, a gate no longer manned by a turbanned guardian. A trespasser in a deserted garden, I stole star-apples from a tree bowed down with fruit; the yellow-green globes ripened and dropped, rotting on the ground.

The grass was long, rank and overgrown, and a broken swing hung by one rope from a high branch of a pepul tree. There was no breeze in the garden and the trapped air smelled of sun-hot greenness. The tree sighed with the weight of the fruit and the silence was broken only by the brain-fever birds – 'brain-fever, brain-fever, brain-*fever*' – that continuous cry on an ever-ascending scale penetrating even a malaria delirium.

I sat screened by the long grass, and across what had become a meadow, the once-grand house lay empty. In this garden a wedding party sat beneath brilliant awnings sewn with braid and tiny mirrors, decorated with garlands. In the house, a child-bride with jewels in her nose and hair, with silver tears painted on her cheeks, waited for her bridegroom. They were gone now, and the garden was sleeping while the star-apples rotted in the grass.

The bridegroom was a big man, big, with a heavy body, and as old as my father. He had a black pencil-line moustache and fat cheeks and he was laughing, waving to friends. Music played. The bride, waiting inside the house, seated on the cool marble floor, in the cool dimness, looked down, her ringed hands still, waiting. And only on that return visit as I recalled the scene, did I realize that real tears escaped from beneath her eyelids, sliding down her cheeks past the painted tears of silver.

*   *   *

Moti was making a real effort to behave like a suburban wife and mother: she went to auctions and bought job lots of second-hand furniture which arrived in pantechnicons, and was left standing in various rooms pending her final decision on where to place it all.

The house was full of this furniture. The plain fact is that there was too much of it: in order to acquire the beds and wardrobes needed for our own use, Moti had also taken delivery of a fumed oak hat-stand and two huge tin trunks filled with 'miscellaneous items'. Her successful bid for the sagging but comfortable sofa and several armchairs (which she planned to have re-covered but never got round to), also brought her a wash-stand, two corner tables and a roll of dusty carpeting. The dining tables and chairs came with a vast, ornate sideboard and several cardboard boxes filled with moth-eaten curtains. And so it went on.

The grand piano she bid for deliberately. We did not need a grand piano. Nor was it cheap. Neither Patrick nor I could play and Moti had forgotten everything except for a blurred approximation of Liszt's *Liebestraume*, but she stood in the doorway of the long sitting room that opened onto the paving stones and the lavender, saw the sun streaming through the leaded windows onto the parquet flooring and said: 'This room must have a piano in it.'

The unwanted items scattered about the house seemed to multiply and grow larger so that in order to cross a room we circumnavigated crates, tea-chests, bookshelves and bedside tables 'surplus to requirements', as the camp notice-board in Poona used to say. But despite the excess, no room in the house was ever completely finished. We pushed things from here to there, trying to make sense of Mo's arbitrary notions of house-furnishing. As we hauled and crashed about, the radio played: 'Music While You Work', 'Workers'

Playtime', 'These You Have Loved', 'Jazz Club', with Stan Kenton (where was he now, the colonel from Chicago who introduced the big band into our lives before joining the legions of the lost?), Duke Ellington and Ella Fitzgerald, even Billie Holiday, though not 'Gloomy Sunday', which I never heard again.

Billie Holiday's dressing room, that first visit, in 1954. Twenty minutes before the concert the room was crowded with well-wishers. It was a small room, hot and smelling of people and booze. The man who took me in, a jazz writer, kissed her and presented her with a bottle of Scotch the way a stage-door Johnny would have flourished a bouquet. He nodded towards me. 'This is Maggie. Great fan of yours.'

She looked at me incuriously, with vague benevolence. The flesh was puffy, the eyes not quite focused: they seemed to swim, darting like fish. She wore thick make-up that stood off her skin, powdery, mauve. Her lipstick was bright scarlet, jammy, over-generously applied.

She nodded, greeting me, and turned away to another arrival, accepting another oblation.

I, too, could have given her a present: I could have told her about listening to that old Columbia 78 on the wind-up gramophone day after day for a year. I would have left out the horrors, the way the words of 'Gloomy Sunday' haunted me. And in any case, that was unimportant now. It was her voice that had survived. I could have said, 'It's because of that song that I'm here today. You changed my life, Billie.' That would have pleased her, surely? 'Hey! Is that right?' She would have laughed, warmed as we always are by such reassurances. The bottle with the individual message is always welcome even when it bobs on a sea of applause.

There was irony here: I could admire Billie, feel

touched by her, feel we had something in common, this woman who looked sick, who lined up the bottles of Scotch in her dressing room and worked her way through them as though they were medicine. Yet for Mo – for *her* bottles – I felt only an unforgiving blank.

Later, in the auditorium, in the spotlight, she was suddenly young and unflawed: in her frock with the off-the-shoulder neckline, teeth gleaming, eyes catching the light, exuding glamour, she reminded me of those women in the Technicolor movies I watched in the air-conditioned Roxy and Trocadero.

The voice, past its best, still worked its old spell. That strange, whining cadence I remembered was even more pronounced, the voice had thinned dangerously, grown grainier, the fragile cascade of notes barely held together. I felt like two bodies in one: I listened and I was up there with her.

Wavering precariously, straining, the voice climbed and clung, reaching for the heart-stopping final note that someone described once as a cry for lost happiness.

But this was much later. It was the music that caused me to jump ahead.

I knew Mo was drinking again – perhaps she had never stopped. The bottles began to pile up in the old familiar way, in wardrobes, linen basket, at the backs of drawers, inside Wellington boots . . .

In one of the empty bedrooms upstairs, the contents of two trunks from an auction covered the floor: mildewed bedlinen, floppy pillows and a collection of *Woman's Weekly* magazine for years past, hundreds and hundreds of them.

There was nothing glossy about *Woman's Weekly*, neither the contents nor the paper it was printed on. The covers always looked the same: blue and a greyish white, with a domestic scene drawn by an artist who specialized in housewives in aprons. These were publications aimed at honest wives and mothers – or at girls planning so to be. They were guides to ordinary, everyday living in a penny-plain Shangri-La. After school I escaped into *Woman's Weekly* land.

The magazines, faded and creased, lay ankle-deep wall to wall. I waded among them, curled up on them, I read them from cover to cover: the recipes, the make-do-and-mend, the problem pages, the knitting patterns (even though I could not knit), everything except the fiction. I tried one or two of the stories but after Boccaccio they seemed a trifle tame, and they certainly bore little resemblance to life as I knew it.

Without servants, without the sun, it was a sad winter for Mo. The house grew dirtier, Patrick went off to London and she grew pinched and querulous: she disliked being left on her own and would have preferred me at home.

'Do you *have* to go to school today?' she would ask, as though to attend every day were somehow excessive.

Dressing hurriedly, terrified she might actually hold me there physically, I escaped to school, to the magic casements, but for me they opened not onto faery lands forlorn, but on to the neatly combed, freshly ironed, onto the exhilaratingly dull, the sunny side of the street. There was no unwashed crockery in Jane Austen; Edith Wharton's interior decorating admitted of no dusty surfaces; one had utter confidence in the social rectitude of Henry James' characters – and the state of his own bathroom. Somewhere in *The Green Hat* Michael Arlen said that conduct was three parts of life. I would have gone further.

Discretion, good behaviour, beautiful manners, understatement and anonymity, these were my goals, threatened when outsiders came too near, as on the day

I brought a friend home to tea. It was unprecedented; one did not bring people home. Home and the people in it were best concealed. But just this once I could not get out of it.

The girls, neat in their gymslips, come through the front door. Maggie, stomach churning, heart thumping, glances quickly around. What will they find? Please God let it be acceptable, let it not be disastrous. Please God let her not be –

From the kitchen she calls to them. The huge round wooden table is untidy, there are crumbs and an unwashed cup or two but nothing too disgusting.

Moti sweeps in: affable, relaxed, greeting the visitor with a smile. Suggesting some melon.

The visitor is astonished. Clearly, she has never been offered melon for tea before. It is exotic, different. Different is just what Maggie does not want to be. Currant buns, peanut butter, bread and jam, these are what people, other people, eat for tea. Cringing inwardly, heart sinking, she grows silent, watches her mother sail off into the kitchen only slightly unsteady on her high heels.

Her friend picks out a tune on the grand piano. Through the half-open door Maggie glimpses Moti taking a quick swig from a bottle behind the cornflakes packet. Back she comes, eyes now at full glitter. Have some more melon. No, Maggie says quickly, but oh yes, please, says the friend.

There is a knife, razor sharp, and Moti slices recklessly, laughing and talking to the girl, not really looking.

Maggie watches in hideous fascination, knowing that at any moment the knife will slice the unprotected thumb, the blood will well up, spurting over the golden flesh of the fruit, there will be melodrama, confusion.

But the fruit is cut and passed across the table, the

163

friend in due course leaves, whispering at the gate, what fun your mother is, Maggie, so amusing, so different. She walks slowly back towards the house. Had the knife slipped, it would have been the cause of embarrassment, shame. Her first thought would have been not for the thumb, sliced and bleeding, but for her own exposed position.

Suddenly she feels ashamed, and decides to thank Moti for making her friend welcome. But Moti is back in the kitchen and reaching behind the cornflakes packet and the moment passes.

Patrick was visiting his family in Ireland. There had been one disastrous encounter with Moti soon after our arrival and it had seemed wisest not to repeat the experiment. Moti, as far as I knew, never took Patrick to meet her mother.

Her father, the eminent architect, had died at some point, or so she said. The abandoned wife remained, but for Moti, with her never-ending quest for a Life of Style, it may simply have proved impossible to introduce as her mother a white-haired old lady in a suburban cottage in an unpicturesque bit of Essex. And her brother – whether alive or killed in action – was clearly dead to her.

So family reunions had no part in our lives. We seemed, rather, to be nomads whose lives consisted of departures interspersed with brief sojourns here and there.

Where are you from? people might ask in conversation. What does one say to that? You mean where was I born? Where was I living last month? Last year? Departures made nonsense of root-growth.

When Moti found she was pregnant it seemed somehow appropriate that a move should be made. Had that not always been the solution? 'Time to move on.' It was not just the pregnancy and the climate; there was also the problem with Patrick's career.

'You're an accountant, not a bloody diplomat!' Moti objected when he raised the subject of professional socializing. But she was wrong: big firms like to feel comfortable with their employees and Patrick's firm was very big indeed. Welcoming him back to the fold after demobilization they expected to welcome his wife. Moti had other ideas.

She gave them one chance: a dinner-dance at the Café Royal. She bought a new dress and went to the hairdresser, and Patrick got out his pre-war evening clothes.

There is no photograph of them preparing to leave for that night, but there is no need of one. I watched them go, climbing into the taxi that was to take them to the station.

Patrick's face shone, as fair-skinned men's do when freshly shaved and bathed. He looked young but already the skin round his eyes was tight and the whites were bloodshot.

His body had altered shape since the suit was made for him, and suits too had changed. It looked clumsy, the jacket too tight, the trousers too wide.

Moti's dress was long, with a halter neck. But money was short and this one was made of cheaper stuff than the midnight blue she had worn to the opera with Alexander.

The cut, too, was less than superb, and her arms, revealed suddenly, looked flabby, her neck scrawny. She had draped her coat round her shoulders. Just as she reached the taxi she remembered some forgotten item and hurried back to the house. Close to, I saw that the line where make-up ended at her jaw was clearly visible; her lipstick, the wrong shade for the current fashion, looked harsh. She grabbed a small bottle of scent from her

165

dressing table and as she turned to leave, caught sight of herself, unprepared, unposed, in the wardrobe mirror.

She stared for a second at what she saw: a tall, ungainly woman with a suburban hairdo, a cheap frock from Oxford Street and a carelessly made up face in which deep lines ran from her nostrils to the corners of her mouth, two more vertically scoring her brow into a permanent frown. She stared, very still, expressionless, then she straightened up, pulled in her stomach, pulled back her shoulders and went past me and out of the house.

I never heard about the evening in detail. 'A bore,' Moti said dismissively. From Patrick I got little more, but piecing things together later I see that it was a marker, a signpost that evening. The Men at the Top saw that Patrick – 'brilliant chap, excellent mind' – who had been considered a young man of promise, might not, after all, quite *do*, further up the ladder. Something . . . unsound about the domestic side? A promotion expected (counted on, financially) went elsewhere. Patrick got into debt. The company was tapped for a loan. Matters deteriorated. Time to move on.

'Australia,' he said enthusiastically. 'We're getting assisted passages; chance of a great future, good climate, lots of swimming, you like swimming, you'll love it.'

'I'm not coming,' I said.

Of course they did not take it seriously at first. I was in their care. A fifteen-year-old child, Moti said, does not make decisions, announcements about her own future.

She was still doing it: I was still old for my age.

'I'm not fifteen, I'm sixteen –'

'What's the difference?'

All the difference. At the Citizens' Advice Bureau they had given me the information I needed: at sixteen, if you had means of support, you could leave home. Or if your parents were leaving, you did not have to go with them. All I had to do was find a job.

166

'I'm staying here.'

It must have been hard for them, puzzling, hurtful, even. They simply could not understand why I wanted to stay behind.

'On your own!' Moti said distractedly. 'What will you do? Work in some shop? What about your dancing? It's unheard of! *Why?*'

Here was the opportunity: now might I do it pat, pour out the years, spare her nothing, tell about the hating, the waiting, the counting. I cast about for the right words, wounding, deadly.

'I'd rather stay here,' I said.

After all, what was the point of words?

Another blur in my memory. Surely the parting was painful? Surely somebody cried? I narrow an inner eye, I strain, but I cannot see them leave.

In the page of memory the departure occurs between the odd and even numbers – there they are, and overleaf, gone. The departure has taken place somehow un-recorded.

The producer was a kind man, tactful when I stopped suddenly in mid-*enchainement* at the audition. It was the pianist who asked, 'D'you sing?'

'Oh yes.'

His hands hovered. 'Go ahead. I'll follow you.'

It was my first professional audition and when I finished, the pianist said, 'Holy shit. Pure Billie.'

I never did follow in Markova's footsteps, not even on the humblest level. Poor Moti: all those years of lessons wasted.

I could have got work as a singer: I had the ear, I had the artistry, even though it was a carbon-copy.

But.

Someone wrote about Billie that singing was the only way she could express how she would like to feel all the time. Letting go and riding the music, I too could glimpse an enchanted country where I could do anything, be anything – flamboyant, dangerous, irresponsible.

But I had spent too many years trying to edge away from centre-stage; there had been too many 'scenes', too many occasions when, thanks to Moti, we drew unwelcome attention to ourselves.

So I mistrusted excess, I was irredeemably unadventurous. The sidelines were more comfortable, the spotlight a sun too fierce for comfort – though now and then, fleetingly, I craved for a glimmer of that spotlight heat to penetrate the day's temperate clime.

It was as a watcher, not a doer; a recorder, not a performer, that I sidled into Billie's world: making the tea, learning the ropes on a weekly jazz journal. It paid no better than the chorus line or clerking, but it was a lot more fun.

Her children treat her as something of a joke, with her anecdotes of legendary figures in small, dark jazz clubs; her fondness for dead people who made records that are all hiss and scratch.

An old song is recorded by a new group and reaches No. 1 in the charts. The boys buy it, play it repeatedly.

'I know that one,' Maggie says, pleased. She hums a few bars. They protest, noisily.

'Mum! D'you mind?'

She is singing it all wrong, they explain. The beat is different now.

They slightly resent the sense of punctuality I have given them: they are not late for appointments, they do not

168

miss trains. But neither do they fuss, as I do, checking time, tickets, passports, obsessively.

When I look back I always seem to find myself somewhere Moti was not; I see myself waiting, unconsulted.

So with me, plans are always discussed at length, examined in detail, decisions put to the vote. They call me the White Rabbit, they find me absurd. And I am absurd. Or rather, this person whom I do not recognize, she is absurd.

They are here and now, putting out new shoots, springing up, magnificent. I am part of the old growth, thickening, no longer green. There are fewer laughs, nothing works out quite as planned. Perhaps I am the White Rabbit.

The boys, at seventeen, are older than I was the last time I saw Moti. I am older than she was then. I thought she was ancient, but now I try to feel how she must have felt: did she have a sense of herself bursting with life, overflowing with untapped promise that no one seemed to see or need?

I realize that by that time I had stopped thinking of her as a dangerous force, as a force of any sort, because I had cut free. So should I mind now, that my children regard me as irrelevant? Is not this how I planned it? To minimize their guilt and their loss, later?

I had hoped, of course, that the early closeness would endure, but they are at the centre of their world, I at its periphery. The death of love and the dimming of passion between consenting adults are familiar causes of lamentation. What is less dwelt on is the rupture between parent and child, the day the child looks at the familiar figure and realizes this is not, after all, God, nor the source of all wisdom and comfort. Is, in fact, irrelevant. Moti must have seen that in my eyes too.

When I married Toby I wrote to Australia and Patrick replied, a nice letter, explaining that things were busy

169

just then, Mo had had two more babies and he was finding it difficult to budget for three children, to keep everything under control. The cost of living had gone up and Moti still liked to have her sprees, he wrote, despite her arthritis growing worse.

'You mother sends her love,' he added. And then, a sort of afterthought, unconnected with what had gone before, 'She tries very hard', he wrote, 'to make a go of things. In her way she's a brave woman.'

Brave?

Locke said children are travellers in a strange country about which they know nothing: is there some other picture hidden under the oils of my portrait of Mo? Is there some alternative narrative that proceeded when my back was turned? When I was looking elsewhere? What I did I *not* know about the woman I hated for so long?

Maybe we should after all, meet again and – *No*. Fear, pain, revulsion, resolution: there will be no meeting. And luckily she is far away.

Patrick wisely signed the letter for both of them: he knew her better than Shorty had.

Curiously, it never surprised me that she stayed married to Patrick, that they remained together in what passed for happiness. On previous experience one might have expected her to move on . . . detach herself, cut and run. But they stayed together and the years passed and one day there came the telegram.

No problem finding me: I was still in the same house, my children know no other.

Was it the ancient Greeks who believed they entered into death backwards, so that what lay before them was their past? It is Moti who has died, but my past as well as hers lies before me.

The telegram is crumpled on the floor, screwed up like a pale, dead flower from a withered garland. There

170

were so many garlands, once, and music. And a harsh, punishing sun. In those early days she used to quote Khayyám when she spoke of her own death, when she made her frequent little threats to end it all: 'Turn down an empty glass . . .'

She came home from one of her jaunts, one of her little sprees, Patrick told me when I telephoned him. She flopped out on the sofa and said it had been a good party. She did not regain consciousness – 'Cerebral haemorrhage,' he said , and added, 'She didn't suffer.'

Once I would have regretted that: why not? She caused suffering enough, why should she escape it at the end? But I found that the object of my hatred for so long, who had returned in nightmares to haunt me year after year ('You were screaming,' Toby used to say, shaking me awake, sleepily hearing yet another tale of Moti), had slipped away without furore, filled not with mortification and regret but Australian wine. Well, why not.

I left the Volvo in the garage and walked to the swimming pool, crowded with schoolchildren and out-of-work actors at this hour, and slid into the water, swallowed up in its cool mouth. I allowed myself to sink to the bottom, the water deepening above my head, the light dimming. My limbs moved slowly, dreamily, I felt my hair lift off my scalp, floating free, a tangle of watersnakes round my head. I hung suspended in the green, roaring silence, waiting to be cleansed, healed of a festering unease.

I stayed down till, lungs bursting, eyes bulging, ears drumming, I shot to the surface, assaulted by a cacophony of childish shrieks, whistles blowing, water slapping noisily against the sides of the pool, the sound re-awakening a long-forgotten echo.

*

It is monsoon time and the rain falls steadily out of the dull yellow-grey sky. Slowly the garden disappears. Amaryllis is an island in a lake of dirty yellow water.

Her father finds an old zinc hip-bath in an outhouse and lifts her carefully into it. It floats! He pushes her round the garden, knee-deep in water, hip-bath bobbing like a wherry, the water slapping and slurping noisily against the sides of the tub. His face is quite close to hers: she sees the skin, toughened by the sun, crease into a smile. She reaches up and touches his cheek, his nose, then she slaps her small hand hard onto the water, soaking his face. He begins to laugh, rocking the boat dangerously. They both laugh, they are yelling with laughter.

It is my only intimate memory of him.

We remember the past in images, but I also remember it in the stab of betrayal – 'But you *promised!*' – in the sound of water, the smell of sunflowers filling hot summer air; the taste of a sweetmeat crumbling on the tongue, stale gin on a woman's breath, the twittering of birds at sundown, the touch of a baby's eyelashes, feather-light against my cheek. The flow of music through the bloodstream.

Some time later I went home: that elusive place, 'home', that always seemed to be somewhere else. A house with long-disused sandpit filled with dead leaves. A house too big for two people and these days it was inhabited mostly by two people.

'I was worried about you,' Toby said.

I handed him the telegram, retrieved from the floor, and he smoothed the crumpled sheet, reading the words.

'All those things about your mother,' he said. 'Is that how it really was?'

The house sat around us, ringing emptily, full of outgrown chambers like a Nautilus shell.

'In some ways,' I said.

The publishers would like to acknowledge permission to reprint lyrics from the following songs:

'Gloomy Sunday' (author: Desmond Carter, composer: Rezsoe Seress), © 1933 Sardas-Zenemuekiado. British publishers: Chappell Music Ltd and Redwood Music Ltd. Used by permission.
'Button Up Your Overcoat' (composers and authors: Ray Henderson/B.G. Bud de Sylva/Lew Brown), © 1928 Redwood Music Ltd. British publishers: Chappell Music Ltd and Redwood Music Ltd. Used by permission.
'Rose Marie' (composer: Rudolf Friml, authors: Oscar Hammerstein II/Otto A. Harbach), © 1924 Harms Inc. British publishers: Chappell Music Ltd and Redwood Music Ltd. Used by permission.
'Good Morning' (composer: Nacio Herb Brown, author: Arthur Freed), © 1939 Chappell & Co. Inc. British publishers: Chappell Music Ltd. Used by permission.